Passion Flower

ALSO BY CYRUS MISTRY

Fiction

Chronicle of a Corpse Bearer

The Radiance of Ashes

Plays

Doongaji House

The Legacy of Rage

CYRUS MISTRY

ALEPH BOOK COMPANY
An independent publishing firm
promoted by ***Rupa Publications India***

Published in 2014 by
Aleph Book Company
7/16 Ansari Road, Daryaganj
New Delhi 110 002

This is a work of fiction. Names, characters, places and incidents are either the product of the author's imagination or are used fictitiously and any resemblance to any actual persons, living or dead, events or locales is entirely coincidental.

ISBN: 978-93-82277-17-0

1 3 5 7 9 10 8 6 4 2

Typeset in Garamond Regular by SÜRYA, New Delhi

Printed and bound in India by Replika Press Pvt. Ltd.

For Adil and Veronik

Contents

Percy

While it was still night in their small cluttered flat the old woman rose quietly and flicked on the harsh, naked light of the overhead bulb. The sleeping figure of her son on the bed parallel to her stirred. Some days she let him sleep longer, till she had lit the stove and put on the kettle. But today, she rudely pulled off the sheet which he had drawn over his head, and called in her throaty, rasping voice:

'Percy! Percy! Are you getting up? Are you awake? I haven't slept all night.'

Percy sat up in bed and groaned, rubbing his eyes. Outside, it was turning grey and birds had begun to chirp softly.

Mother and son went about their morning chores and ablutions silently. Banubai lit the wick stove and put the kettle on. Percy took in the milk bottle from the verandah, switched off the night lamp and proceeded to fold the sheets. Then, using a polythene hose fitted with a nozzle, Percy filled water in the large plastic drum and brass pots in the kitchen and bathroom. The plastic nozzle had become loose, and the force of the water in the tap created a fountain of spray which drenched his shirt and wetted the floor all around him. While the steaming water in the soot-blackened kettle soaked in the colour of tea leaves, the old woman and her son stood outside on the verandah facing east, flicking their kashtis and reciting their morning prayers. When they had finished, Banubai noticed that his sudrah was very damp, and she made him change it; Percy was prone to colds.

After tea, Banubai and Percy swept and swabbed the three small rooms and kitchen of their flat (Banubai had long ago decided to dispense with servants, whose slave she didn't want to be), taking turns with the broom and mop. Next, from her collection of rangoli boxes the old woman selected a little one, perforated with the outlines of a pair of fish, and printed patterns of chalk on the threshold of every doorway. By now the coals on the fire would be hot and sparking. Using a pair of pincers, Banubai arranged them carefully on the afarghan and sprinkled them with incense dust. Then, raising the silver smoking receptacle high in the air, and mumbling her prayers softly, the small figure of Banubai walked through their rooms, circumnavigating the many old pieces of furniture, fumigating every corner with the incense smoke, dispelling the last vestiges of night and ungodliness from their homestead. She had had a traditional upbringing. She liked to do everything right, the way it was prescribed by her ancestors. Ever since her husband died, eighteen years ago, there had been no one to prevent her from doing things just right: the way she liked to do them.

Soon it would be time for Percy to leave for work. The firm of Bhairam Cheliram & Sons Pvt Ltd opened early, at a half past eight, and closed at half past four. He had been working there for the last fifteen years, first as delivery boy, and now as Chief Clerk (as it happened, there *was* only one clerk employed by the firm).

Percy was thirty-four, and was going to turn thirty-five next month, but Banubai didn't trust him to fry his own eggs for breakfast.

'You'll splash hot oil on yourself, you ninny. Don't even try!' she had said cuttingly the only time he had put the frying pan on the stove to make his own breakfast. 'And how much oil! Marere mua, you've finished half my tin! Do you know how much this one tin costs?' She bullied him too much, she sat on his head. He knew it. Sometimes, in his heart, he rebelled against her tyranny, her strict routines. But he never spoke his resentment. It was better to be obedient if you were a duffer. And Percy had had long training in servility. Maybe he could have managed quite well on his own, better than she thought he could. But he wasn't sure. He had never been without her, and the thought had never occurred to him that he might, some day.

Half an hour later, as Percy was getting dressed to leave for office, he discovered there wasn't a single button on his trouser flies. His other two pairs were with the dhobi.

'Mumma!' he called out to Banubai in his flutey, quavering voice. 'Mumma, *all* my buttons are gone. Not one left. Stitch me some now, will you? How can I go like this?'

'My eyes don't work so well anymore. Haven't I told you, start doing things with your own hands now. How much can one person do? I have but two hands,' Banubai harangued her son. 'If something happens to me tomorrow, God forbid, what will become of you? Give, give. . . Bring needle and thread. And my specs.'

Her protestations notwithstanding the short and wiry

Banubai, who was sixty-eight, was very active still. Holding the needle within an inch of her nose, she threaded it skillfully, at the first try. Then, bending over the trousers, she muttered under her breath, softly but audibly, 'Where will I find you a wife? Who will marry you, a chap like you . . .?'

And Percy, who was standing beside her in his shirt and his shoes, with a towel wrapped around his midriff declared, 'I don't want anyone, Mumma, I don't want! I'll stay here with you. You can look after me better than any wife.'

'Ja, ja gadhera! Show some sign of brains when you open your mouth,' Banubai shouted at him; but it was playful ire, and a half smile diffused her grouch of concentration.

As soon as Percy left the house, Banubai retired to the kitchen and began furiously to knead the dough which she had left overnight in a wet cloth. She had an order to meet today, for one dozen popatjis and two dozen bhakhras. Three times a week, on Tuesdays, Thursdays and Fridays, Banubai walked from door to door in her own colony and to neighbouring Parsi homes, with a bag full of doughnuts, pickles, sweet malido, spicy vasaanu, and other homemade delicacies, which she sold at a modest price, in this way supplementing Percy's small income.

~

Percy Bhathena was a decidedly odd-looking fellow, and he knew it very well. The many large mirrors at home had impressed the fact indelibly upon his consciousness. How many hours had he spent gazing at the pointed end of his long head, which was covered with a thick, bristly growth that reminded him of the quills of a porcupine? How many painful moments squeezing out the blackheads and boils on his cheeks and nose—but they always came back. The rest of his body was smooth and fairly hairless. Tall and thin, hunched and sallow, his small, mean-looking face sported a fungoid growth of thin wispy curls, and a faint moustache, which had never known the cutting edge of a razor. His mother had forbidden him to shave, on the grounds that it was unnecessary in his case. She disliked men with thick growths, like his deceased father, Boman Bhathena, who for fifteen years had unfailingly shaved every morning *after*, instead of before, his bath, as any civilized, self-respecting Parsi would—in this way, daily polluting their hearth and home, merely to spite his wife and ridicule her beliefs.

Every time Percy was obliged to negotiate the wide colony compound, lined on both sides by residential blocks, a terrible feeling of awkwardness invaded his limbs, his shoulders, his hands, his neck, his feet—as though each of these had acquired some measure of autonomy from his sense of physical co-ordination and ease. The result was a comical and ludicrous gait, not unlike that of a camel. The residents of Batliwalla Villa, the small Parsi colony at the end of Sleater Road, had always regarded the boy (even now they were unable to think of him as a grown man) with some pity and much amusement. Percy had no truck with any of them. He lived like an outcast in the colony, and regarded some of his neighbours with positive trepidation even though for many years now they had left him alone.

The same people who had tormented his boyhood and

youth, had by now written him off as a 'gone case', and barely permitted him a smile of recognition. For years, they had made him the butt of their jokes, their lewdness, their nastiest pranks. He was their punching bag, their errand boy, their coolie, repository of their most depraved fantasies, their vilest abuse. None of it had seemed to daunt Percy. No matter what names you called him, no matter how hard you twisted his arm, Percy was always willing to smile and bow and flatter his enemies, pretend that his persecutors were really his playmates, and that the scourging he was receiving was only a measure of his popularity, a game which allowed everyone to have a good time. From an early age, Percy had learned the trick of the ingratiating smile. In school, as at home, he had suffered daily castigation at the hands of his masters and his mates, who would pursue him and shower him with a rain of blows at the slightest pretext. Servility and clowning, he realized, were his safest options. If he could make his tormentors laugh they let him off more easily. What was it about him that incited and irked people so? What worm-like qualities did he exhibit that invited people to trample on him? His mirrors had provided no answer to this enigma.

Most of the colony wildcats had since satiated or sublimated their sadistic longings. They had made respectable marriages and now held responsible jobs. They had no time for Percy. But some of the older residents, with long memories, felt genuine sympathy for Boman's boy. They remembered what they thought of as the 'root cause', the shameful marital discord between Boman and Banu, of which the boy was an obvious casualty. Every time they saw him skulking past their porches, where they reclined in their easy chairs, they shook their heads and murmured, 'See what a tight grip she has kept on his reins still. Hasn't let an inch slip. What a namby-pamby she's made him into, poor duffer . . .' And they remembered his father, the jolly, fun-loving Boman Bhathena, who had entered into such an unpropitious and unhappy marriage, and paid for it with his life.

Boman Bhathena had been a part-time insurance agent and a racehorse buff, who was known to have won and squandered thousands of rupees in a single weekend. Not to speak of his marathon nights at the card table with his jockey friends, from whom he picked up tips for forthcoming racing events. Boman took no pains to conceal his disgust for his wife. Many times, at drinking parties which went on till morning, he had publicly disowned his son for being a sissy and a true son of his mother. Boman could not brook any of Banu's religious nonsense and he fancied himself as something of an iconoclast. Banu was willing to tolerate everything else, but his spitefulness and profanity frightened her. She bided her time; till the blow came, from Above.

One day, when Percy was only thirteen, he was summoned out of class and sent home. When he got to the flat he found the front door crowded with neighbours who made way for him. Inside, he saw his mother crying, and his father stretched out on his bed under a white sheet. His usually ruddy face was pale, his stubble unshaven, his eyelids shut forever. Boman Bhathena had been a big man, powerfully built, a voracious meat-eater, whose chronic complaint had been constipation. He would spend many hours every morning, pacing about, drinking endless cups of tea. Then he would lock himself in their toilet, and their small flat would resound with the echoes of his loud cursing and groaning, sometimes rewarded by sighs of relief. But this morning, Boman's reward had been of a more permanent nature. Banubai had been alarmed when she heard his straining and swearing something frightful, like an enraged bull. Suddenly, there was a cry, and then a soft thump followed by silence. It took the neighbours two hours to unhinge the solid teak door. By then, his body had already begun to stiffen. The doctor's conclusion was that death had been almost instantaneous, caused by the rupture of a blood vessel in Boman's brain, due to too much straining over the pot.

That was the end of Percy's academic career. His mother had no choice but to withdraw him from school and find him a job.

The firm of Bhairam Cheliram & Sons Pvt Ltd was the sole manufacturer and distributor of two time-tested and time-honoured Unani compounds called *Teston 30* and *Test-up Royale*, guaranteed to restore the flagging virility of any male. *Test-up Royale* was the more potent version of the two, and cost twenty rupees extra.

Percy was in charge of filling the challans and invoices, dispatching the required cartons with the delivery boys as per the number of orders received daily, and ensuring that there was no pilferage or breakage which the boys were not called to account for. It was a simple but responsible job. Seth Bhairam himself handled the cash receipts, but in his absence, Percy was expected to take over. The office was located at Princess Street, and in many ways, it represented a haven of peace and stability for Percy. Here, he conducted himself with authority and dignity. He worked hard and efficiently, and tried to be fair towards everyone. He was aware that some of the delivery boys sniggered and invented uncomplimentary names for him, but this was a small vexation which he could afford to ignore. Because the boys knew as well as he did, that he had real power over their jobs. The Seth depended on Percy, and liked him well.

Seth Bhairam Cheliram was a forthright man with a booming voice, sturdily-built, self-made, a hirsute septuagenarian, who always wore a clean white kurta and a fine muslin dhoti. The dhoti's translucence was ill-equipped to conceal a large, pendulous object whose stupendous contours were clearly visible for all who cared to look, and served as a kind of living advertisement for the Seth's restorative concoctions. One day, shortly after his appointment as Chief Clerk, Percy was summoned to the Seth's office with his ledgers. The Seth asked him to pull up a chair and be seated beside him. Together, they peered into the ledgers. Seth Bhairam was very pleased with the way records had been maintained. He placed an appreciative hand on Percy's thigh, and began to gently squeeze and massage it; then slowly, the hand crept upwards to his crotch. Percy was ashamed, yet curiously grateful for the touch. When the Seth's fingers began to fiddle with his buttons, he wanted to say, 'No! Please, enough . . .' but he remained silent. Words had never come easily to Percy, especially when he most urgently needed them.

The shrill bell of the telephone on the Seth's desk made both of them start. The Seth disengaged his hand and answered the phone. Something which the caller said infuriated him, and he started shouting into the phone in guttural Kutchchi. In the middle of his red-faced deposition, he suddenly stopped and dismissed Percy with a wave of his hand. That was four years ago. The incident had never repeated itself.

At four-thirty, or a quarter to five, Percy left the office and caught a bus for home. His mother made him a cup of tea and gave him something to eat. Then she went out for about two hours, to the neighbourhood fire temple. It was usually quite deserted at this time. She sat there alone and prayed fervently, with a clean heart, gazing into the Holy Fire (she knew many long passages from memory and did not always need to refer to her prayerbook). When she had finished, she always felt so light and relieved. Then, usually, she stopped to chat with the mobeds, young boys and old men in crumpled white gowns, who lazed on the front benches after their day's labours.

These two hours were Percy's own, his very own, and for years he hadn't known how to spend them. In his younger days, in the evenings, he would always be found at the colony clubhouse. This was really just a small room which had been set aside to provide recreation to the tenants, in the form of one carom board with coins and striker, and two packs of cards. There was a heavy demand for use of the carom board and Percy, like the others, always eagerly awaited his turn to play. He was not a good player, though, and the three others who found themselves on the same board would argue about who should partner him. In the end they would draw lots to arrive at a decision.

One day, an unpleasant incident occurred. While trying to execute a particularly complicated rebound shot, Percy hit the striker with so much force and angularity that it flew into the air, bounced off the inner edge of the carom board, and struck his partner squarely on the jaw. The fury and indignation of the aggrieved player was more than matched by the uproar of the observers, who had discovered an unmistakable scratch on the board, where the striker had bounced. They roughly unseated the defacing culprit by first toppling his chair, then pummeling him all the way to the door, while listing a range of unpleasant consequences he was likely to face, should they ever again find him seated at the carom board.

So the problem of what to do with his evenings remained. Until, one day, Percy remembered his father's old hand-wound gramophone.

Twenty years had passed since Boman died. Everything in the flat had changed, hardly any evidence remained that a man by that name had once lived there, and sired a boy called Percy. One old photograph, which Banubai had got framed, hung on the wall; a few dinner suits were preserved in mothballs, in the upper part of a cupboard which was not used anymore; and, on top of the same cupboard, stacked under a mass of cobwebs, was the gramophone, and a box of records. Why had he never thought of it before? Percy got it down, dusted it, wiped a record, wound the key, and lo! it still worked. Percy was delighted, enraptured, ecstatic. From that evening onwards, he knew what he wanted to do with his time. He plunged headlong into an adventure in music which was sensual, voluptuous almost; he discovered new worlds in those thirty-odd shellac discs, which gave meaning and strength and calm to his floundering, timid soul (despite the fact that his choice of listening pleasure, as it were, was proscribed by his father's tastes, and the tastes of another era).

Percy was charmed and entranced by 'The Merry Widow', 'The Maid of the Mountains', 'No, No, Nanette'. He was electrified by Derek Oldham's rendition of the 'Indian Love Call' and the 'The Donkey Serenade' from the film (so the label said), *Firefly*. He wondered about all these old films which he had never seen, how beautiful they must have been. From the distant recesses of his memory, a vision flashed upon him of his father gesturing expansively, glass in hand, as he sang an imitation of Bing Crosby's 'Don't Fence Me In'; and now he heard the original again. He felt a tremendous surge of energy and passion, every time he heard Arthur Tracy (*The Street Singer*) recounting his experiences 'In A Little French Casino'. There were also the Viennese waltzes of Strauss and Lehar, innumerable foxtrots, tangos, rumbas. There was Liszt's Hungarian Rhapsody No. 2 and 'Die Fledermaus', an album of K.L. Saigal's and three or four medleys of Parsi gumbhar songs.

Every evening, as soon as his mother left for the Atash Behram, the gramophone would come down from the cupboard. Of course, it was ancient, the needles were all worn, the pick-up raced through the record like a hacksaw and sounded like one, too; and in the background there was a constant, awful, ominous crackling, accompanied by the repeated thud of the needle against the catch-groove. None of this mattered. Percy would listen to the records over and over again, unmindful of the quality of reproduction, until it was time for his mother to return.

One day, while passing by a pavement bookstall at Kalbadevi,

Percy saw a tattered copy of Bingham's *Ballroom Dancing Made Easy* (with simple diagrams), and the thought occurred to him that, if he ever married, he might want to dance with his bride on their wedding night. So he bought the book for two rupees and learnt the basic steps of the waltz and the foxtrot. The rumba and the tango, the samba and the cha-cha, these looked impossibly complicated and Percy could not unravel the diagrams at all. But with the waltz and the 'fox', when he felt he had mastered the steps and learnt the knack of moving in time, he decided to try them out to music.

The first sessions were tremendously exhilarating. Percy whirled and glided and executed difficult turns and pirouettes, and bowed graciously to his partner before and after every dance. Inevitably, one evening, bubbling with excitement, Percy unlocked the cupboard which contained his father's suits. One immediately attracted him—a navy blue with velvet lining, the colour of red wine. The trousers were too big for him at the waist, but he held them up with a belt. The jacket made him look stuffy and puffed-up, but Percy was impressed by the shoulder-pads, which disguised his thinness and gave him stature. The sleeves were a little too long.

For several weeks, this became his joyous pastime—to listen to the music and *dance*. When he danced, magnificent in his father's suits, Percy did not dance in the brief circumference of open space bounded by the beds, the sofa and front door. He danced in a vast, resplendent ballroom on tiles of marble, and moved with the grace and lilt of romance. In his arms, he held his wife, his first love, a fair and elegant beauty with a small nose and a dimpled chin.

Before Banubai returned from the Atash Behram, Percy changed into his own clothes and stowed the gramophone and records back upon the cupboard. When she got back she would immediately go in to warm the food, and they sat down to an early dinner. After dinner, Percy washed the dishes, while Banubai glanced through the day's *Jame*.

Hardly ten or fifteen minutes later, the lights in the Bhathena household were extinguished and the room where they slept would be bathed in the ghastly phosphorescence of the orange night-lamp above their beds.

But how long can a young man remain cooped up indoors with his dreams? The ballroom of romance cannot be conjured up daily, no matter how valiant the spirit that dreams it, how forlorn the heart that craves it.

Some evenings, in desperation, Percy would leave the house and take long bus rides through the city, from terminal to terminal—just to be out in the open, in the midst of other people. But often, as he watched dusk settle over the city from his window-seat, his inner voice would engage him in such captivating dialogues that Percy would be lost to the world. Until a sharp jolt or swerve of the bus awakened him to the stares of his fellow passengers, and he realized he had been muttering to himself, perhaps even gesticulating with those hands which now lay docile in his lap.

At other times, if a young woman happened to sit on the same seat beside him, Percy would long to speak to her, his heart pounding with a frightening momentum, his upper lip moist, his mouth bitterly dry.

Was it mere chance that made you sit beside me? Listen, please, I have something to say . . . I cannot bear to think that in a few moments you may reach your destination and I will never see you again . . . Hear me out, I cannot harm you with my words . . . You are the most beautiful woman I have ever seen . . . You are more beautiful than anyone or anything on this earth. . . Come. . . Come closer, my love, my angel . . . Don't be afraid . . .

But words never came easily to Percy, especially when he most urgently needed to speak. Instead, they hammered and ricocheted inside the walls of his head, like the desperate cry of a thwarted telepathist.

~

It was while travelling in a bus one evening that Percy learnt of the existence of an organization which called itself The Bombay Gramophone Society. A postcard lying near his feet from the general secretary of the body to one of its members, a Mr D.S. Siganporia of Bazaargate, Fort, informed him of the venue, date and time of a forthcoming annual general body meeting of the Society.

Percy was terribly excited by this fortuitous discovery. The Bombay Gramophone Society! Were there others like him then, who had actually formed a society, who congregated on certain fixed days at an appointed hour with their gramophones and their records, and danced late into the night in their dinner suits and tuxedos? Percy resolved to attend the general body meeting to find out more about the society, and whether it would accept him as a member.

The Bombay Gramophone Society conducted its listening

sessions on the premises of a public library, on Wednesdays and Saturdays at 6.30 p.m., after the library's closing hours. The library authorities had kindly permitted the use of a section of their reference hall which contained enough chairs to accommodate all the members. In front of the dozen rows of chairs were placed two large speakers, connected to a record player which was concealed behind the first of the tall bookshelves.

Most of the fifteen or twenty members who attended the listening sessions quite regularly, were well-to-do, retired, elderly folk, all serious lovers of Western classical music. Some of them probably owned sophisticated hi-fi systems and had private collections of records at home. But the society served as a club which provided for a quiet evening's outing, a meditative and enriching two hours of listening to the world's greatest music and an occasion to share the prized highlights of their personal collections with their co-members. The annual membership fee was only twelve rupees, and the society welcomed new members.

On the day of the annual general body meeting, Percy arrived late; he had been misdirected by a pedestrian and had had some difficulty finding the library. He entered the reference hall and sat quietly in the last row. No one turned to look at him, nobody noticed him at all. The meeting was in a state of excited disarray, and three or four members were trying to speak at the same time. An elderly gentleman was holding the floor and hoarsely demanding an assurance from the general secretary, one Mr Dholakia, that their monthly programmes would be mailed on time in future. Others took up for Dholakia and asked the speaker to explain how he could hold the secretary responsible for delays in the postal services. Yet others pointed out that the speaker, whose name seemed to be Shroff, never attended meetings in any case, so who was he to complain about the programmes reaching him too late?

Percy's initial disappointment was crushing. Of course there was not going to be any dancing here. Most of these old dodderers could barely walk, let alone dance. What a waste of time, he thought, listening to them argue. He felt a strong urge to get up and leave. But the music equipment, especially the tall speakers, exerted a mesmeric effect on him, which kept him seated. He had never seen such big ones before. When the meeting came to an end with the reading of the minutes of the last meeting, the gathered company settled down to a hushed silence; and when the music began, every one of Percy's objections melted away and became utterly irrelevant. Percy was transported. At the end of the evening's programme, Percy paid his membership fee. The treasurer introduced him to the office-bearers and three or four of the senior members. Each time he presented 'Mr Bhathena, our new member,' he made the same remark about how happy he was that some 'young blood' was being infused into 'our old society'.

Now, at last, Percy's life was imbued with a sense of purpose and belonging. Every Wednesday and Saturday, without exception, he would arrive early and pace about the library's foyer, waiting for the programme to begin. As the other members started arriving, they would greet him politely and respectfully. They were impressed with his ardour for music which was reflected in his unflagging attendance at the meetings of the Society, but they were secretly amused by the size of his suits and the pomposity of his manner and bearing. At 6.30 p.m. sharp, the general secretary, Mr Dholakia, would disappear behind the bookshelves; then a pregnant crackling silence would ensue; and in a moment, the devoted audience would be launched on a deep and stirring emotional journey, while the great masters of world music painted their spiritual canvases of life's defeats and despairs, agonies, ecstasies, triumphs.

Percy was deeply moved and disturbed by the music he heard twice a week under the auspices of the Bombay Gramophone Society. There had been nothing like it in his father's collection. Cyclostyled programme notes were distributed before the evening's session began and, gradually, Percy began to discern differences of style, between Beethoven and Vivaldi, between Mozart and Mendelssohn. He even developed his own tastes and preferences. Percy was particularly touched by Brahms, especially his great violin concerto, the operas of Puccini, the dark rumblings of Sibelius.

In the middle of the evening, there would be an intermission of ten minutes, during which members would chat convivially with one another. They would compare notes about forthcoming music recitals in the city, discuss which of them promised to be exciting, and urge one another not to dally about booking their tickets. Percy picked up the knack of joining in these desultory conversations. He had made quite a few acquaintances among the society's members—the portly Mr Sanjana, who was very reserved but kind; old Mrs Anklesaria, who used a walking-stick and brought her aged manservant along as an escort; jolly old Gorwalla, who sometimes came for meetings bursting with hives; and hoarse Fardoon Umrigar, who brought up so much phlegm that he frequently had to tip-toe away in the middle of a piece to expectorate—and during the intermission, Percy would lean across to one of them and remark, 'So, have you got your tickets for that Russian pianist at Patkar? I believe next month there is that French ballet troupe coming too . . .'

One Saturday evening, during intermission, Percy was pacing quietly up and down the passage area behind the chairs; his head bent forward, his hands behind his back. He had just heard a selection of Chopin nocturnes. They had lulled and soothed him, and made him feel curiously despondent. One of the pieces had evoked for him a smell, an odour which he could not place but seemed to know from very long ago. The memory of that unmistakable smell nagged him still, as he paced, waiting for the next item on the programme, a piece with a promising title: 'Invitation to the Dance' by Carl Maria von Weber.

Suddenly, Mrs Anklesaria, that eccentric old dowager, turned and called out sternly, from where she sat in the first row:

'Mr Bhathena! Why are you flitting about back there like a ghost? Please be seated. You are making me *very* nervous . . .'

A few members tittered at this outburst. Mrs Anklesaria's description of him had stung Percy, and he wanted to retort with something equally sharp and stinging. But he bowed courteously and, without a word, went back to his seat. In any case, it was time for the programme to resume.

But that evening, when the programme came to an end, and the members dispersed one by one, Percy met a real ghost in the library toilet. He had gone in to take a leak. When he finished, he found that the bolt on the door of his cubicle had jammed. After five anxious minutes of struggling with it, the door finally opened. When he stepped out, he saw a young man, about his own age, combing his hair in front of the mirror above the wash-basins. Again that smell, so strong this time: the smell of sogginess and swamp. Now he remembered it clearly, and turned pale. Why . . . but, by God! . . . it was—the name escaped Percy's lips with a fearful gush of emotion—

'Dara!'

The figure did not turn, but merely met his eyes in the mirror and stopped combing. There was a twinkle in those eyes. It *was* Dara. He had grown somehow, his body had aged. But this is what he would have looked like if he had lived. Dara had been his only real friend at school. He had died in a drowning accident, during a class picnic at Powai Lake. His classmates had egged him on into the waters. His bloated body, entwined in weed and sedge, was recovered by local fishermen after an hour-long search; it was then loaded on to the school-bus by the driver and their horrified schoolmaster, Mr Braganza, on whom it fell to break the news to Dara's parents.

'It *is* you,' Percy whispered.

'Same old Percy . . . How your stomach churned in there just now when the door stuck,' the ghost of Dara chuckled. 'Gave you a real fright, didn't I?'

Percy could hardly believe his ears. But he was not in the least frightened. On the contrary, a strange and intoxicating excitement bubbled and coursed through his veins, like rising laughter.

‘I had always thought I would be terrified if I ever met a real ghost. But with you, it’s different. You are my friend, Dara . . .’ Percy held out his arms and approached his dead friend offering an open embrace. Dara remained impassive, and frowned. In that moment, a strong stench of swamp hit him, and Percy did not move any closer.

‘Talk to me, say something,’ he urged. ‘What are you doing here, Dara, of all places? Do you come here like me to listen to music?’

‘I listen sometimes,’ answered the spectre grimly. ‘Most of the time it’s a bloody nuisance. I like it here. I feel the need to complete my education.’

Percy was touched. He remembered that his friend had always been of a scholastic bent of mind. Such perseverance. . .

‘But Dara, after all these years. . .why have you come now? Why do you show yourself to me now? There were other times when I missed you, longed for you, when I needed you so much. Why now?’

‘I’ve been watching you, Percy! I’ve been watching you for weeks now!’ Dara’s voice in the small toilet sounded wrathful and thunderous; disembodied, as if the figure standing there moving his lips was only a prop. ‘You bloody moron! Sometimes when I see you, I feel like grabbing you by the shoulders and shaking you till your teeth rattle. You’re still the same maaderchod ghelo you always were. Wake up! What’s with you? We don’t have forever. Time is running out, for all of us . . . And let me tell you what I ’pecially came to say: you look *ridiculous* in those moth-eaten suits. Can’t you find anything else to wear?’

Then the figure of his dead friend, his best friend, whom he had somehow inexplicably angered, began to fade before his eyes.

'Dara, I love you! Don't go yet! I love you,' Percy cried. Perhaps in response to this appeal the apparition's gradual dissolution into nothingness hesitated momentarily. Dara's voice rang out again, this time wobbly, incorporeal, as if from very far.

'I love you too, Percy. Always did. What good does that do us now? Finally, it's each to himself. You could not stop me from drowning, could you, while you watched, screaming your lungs out on shore? Take care, Percy. Look after yourself. And listen, old chap, I think you'd better be rushing home, now. Your mother doesn't have much longer to live.'

With these words, the ghost of Dara vanished in thin air. And Percy found his own face staring back at him in the bathroom mirror.

His mind was in a whirl, he could hardly walk straight. The library's watchman who had been waiting for him to emerge from the bathroom glared at him suspiciously, and muttered something rude. For only the second or third time in his life, Percy hailed a cab and directed the driver to take him to Sleater Road. The taxi cruised along Marine Drive at a leisurely pace. Percy wanted to say: *Drive faster. I'm in a hurry, that's why I hired your cab.* But he could not speak. He crouched in the back seat, shivering, reciting fervent Ashem Vahus and Yatha Ahu Vairyos silently.

When he reached Batliwalla Villa, he saw from a distance that the lights in his flat were on, as usual. He raced to the door and lightly jabbed the electric buzzer. His mother threw open the door.

'Where were you! Do you have any notion of the time?' she demanded, not waiting to hear his reply. 'I've eaten. Your dinner will be ice-cold by now.'

'But Mumma,' Percy asked in a shaky voice, 'you are feeling okay, no? Your health . . .'

'Mua, are you waiting for me to fall sick or what?' Banubai asked irritably. 'What's the matter, why are you trembling like that? You look like you've just seen a ghost. Oh go on,' said Banubai, climbing into bed. 'Go in and eat your food. And put off this light.'

A tremendous feeling of reprieve, of divine clemency surged through Percy as he sat down to dinner. But he was puzzled. A question kept repeating itself in his head: why would an apparition lie?

Banubai had cooked his favourite dish, papeta nu gos, but he swallowed it disinterestedly, without enjoyment, as if it were plain cabbage.

For days the horrible prophecy haunted Percy, and he watched his mother covertly for signs of ill-health or impairment. But she seemed strong and active as ever. Then, one morning, two weeks later, Percy received a phone call at his office from one of the neighbours, asking him to come home immediately. He did not need to question her about the reason for this strange demand. He replaced the receiver without a word, and began to weep like a child.

Once again, Percy took a taxi home, this time urging the driver, 'Jaldi, jaldi . . .' to which the driver retorted, 'But you can see there's traffic blocking my way . . .' Percy knew it was no use hurrying, it was already too late. He understood at last why Dara had come to him, and he felt immense gratitude for his forewarning. Now he had to be strong. For Dara's sake, for his own.

'Here he is,' the neighbours called, seeing him approach. They surrounded him and led him into his own flat. Inside, he saw what he had expected to see. He flung himself on the floor beside the bed on which his mother lay, and pulled off the sheet which covered her; as she had so many time unsheeted him at daybreak, to make him rise and fill the drums with water. He put his arms around her and began to blubber, 'Mumma, Mumma . . .' The neighbours restrained him and caressed his back with soothing hands.

'Dikra, we all have to go,' they consoled, 'some day or other.'

Goolmai and Sheramai and Dossa and Fariburz recreated for him Banubai's last hour, how she had looked, what she had said . . . for she had visited all their homes on her round, before collapsing in C Block, outside the door of the Karanjias, after climbing three floors with a bagful of foodstuffs. Doctor Pardiwalla had come and gone. There was nothing he could do, except certify her death.

'We have arranged everything,' the neighbours reassured him. 'Don't have one worry. Fali has booked a bungli, Dorab has gone to the *Jam-e-Jamshed* office to give an insertion. The hearse will be here about two. Don't worry, later we'll see about everything else, too. This is our duty as neighbours . . . Go, you go in and wash your face, and then lie down for a little while.'

Percy was overwhelmed by their kindness and sympathy. He basked in its warmth and felt cleansed by his sorrow, and by their love. At last, he felt, they had accepted him. He forgave them everything, everything from the past that they and their children had inflicted on him. The past didn't matter anymore. Everything had changed now. There was a spare cot in the next room. Percy followed their advice and went in to lie down.

But he could not rest. His mind danced like a flame in a strong breeze. Strange thoughts, inappropriate to his hour of grief, flooded him, alongside the image of his mother's ashen face, her jaw tied with a strip of cloth, her eyelids slightly ajar. These thoughts seemed vaguely improper to him, because they concerned themselves with change, so soon after Banubai was gone, but he could not resist them. He rearranged the furniture in his head, he decided to throw open all the windows in their rooms which had remained permanently shut because Banubai couldn't stand draughts. He must join the two beds now, so he could roll and sprawl over them as he liked. He would ask the milkman not to ring the doorbell, so he could sleep longer. If he could find a good tailor to alter his father's suits . . . Oh Mumma! Every now and then, his tears would begin to flow again, but with them came a sense of release, and a calm which he had never experienced before . . . Suddenly, Percy sat up in bed. A tune was ringing in his head. He had never had a good memory for music, but now he remembered the entire melody, which he had heard just once, two weeks ago. It was Weber's 'Invitation to the Dance'.

A few minutes or few hours later, when Goolmai, the next-door neighbor, came in to call him, she found Percy circling the floor, his face flushed and strangely radiant. She was startled by the gleam in his eyes and the fact that he bowed when he saw her, graciously, as though he were—good God!—as though he were asking her for the pleasure of this dance! Poor, poor wretch, feeble-brained always, had he lost his mind completely now? But she hid her shock, ignored the arms outstretched in her direction, and only said, 'The hearse has arrived, Percy.'

As in confirmation, the old pendulum clock in the room wheezed and whirred and tolled twice.

Unexpected Grace

I am alone here. At least, alone in my wakefulness.

My husband has his back to me. It's a habit with him. He cannot sleep unless he turns away. Just now, I could have sworn I heard him snoring. The next moment he rasped aloud: 'Just listen to that bloody racket!' and pulled his pillow more firmly over his upturned ear. That's another curious habit of his. He uses his pillow to cover his head rather than to lie on. What's he trying to muffle? The humming of crickets? The clatter of his lascivious dreams? His awareness of my presence at his side?

Ours is a very quiet residential colony. After dusk, a thick soft silence descends on it like a blanket. Tonight, the cats are on heat. In our bedroom, under the glow of the golden yellow night-lamp we had installed at the same time as Baby's crib, their shrieking and wailing sounds positively ghoulish. My husband doesn't like cats. I listen intently . . . That cry! So much like Fuzzy. The same aggressive, hoarse, shrill, wildly modulating, gently simmering scream of seduction—or is it grief, a kind of mourning at the body's compulsions?—but I know it can't be him. My poor Fuzzy is a thousand miles away in Bombay.

He was packed off when I got pregnant. Doctor's orders,

strongly seconded by my husband: the risks of feline infections to the unformed embryo are numerous. Mother agreed to keep him. My child was born normal. No missing toes, no blindness, no harelip, none of those things that could have happened if I had kept Fuzzy. So I have a child now, and no Fuzzy. Why is there always such a price to pay for everything? The cats are still singing their desire with coloratura abandon. I climb out of bed and go to the window.

Our colony looks so pretty, especially on a chilly, misty night like this. The well-paved walks, through wooded lots and open grounds dividing the elegant bungalows, are neither too brightly lit, nor looming with great shadows that harbour unseen pitfalls, inexplicable fears. It's all so lovely and calm and vast. Yet barren, devoid of feeling. I have no friends here. The neighbours stay aloof. Even the servants seem to know we are not quite so wealthy as their other employers. Even they belong here in a way I cannot. It's different with my husband. His one driving ambition is to be able to hobnob on an equal footing with the colonels and ambassadors and ex-nawabs who are our fellow residents. As for my own ambitions, I hardly know what they are. My life is incomplete. I've been robbed of my sovereignty. Do I dare spell out what is lacking? What is it my husband has, and other normal people have, that I do not? Do I know? I have always wanted a child, always believed I would be wonderfully happy if I had one. My cats and other pets were surrogates, I thought. Now I have a child. This is how I feel. I am bereaved. I am shorn. I am naked in the cold.

Thud, thud, the watchman saunters stiffly past the front of the house, his head wrapped in a muffler, tapping his staff on the ground. He is staring directly at me. He slows down, but does not stop. He continues staring at this figure in the window, enveloped in yellow haze, even when he has to turn his neck to do so. Does he think he has seen a burglar? Or a ghost? Does he think the house is smouldering, about to erupt in flames? Raise the alarm, summon the other watchmen. All is not well here. I don't blame you if you think so. It is 3 a.m. I move away from the window and stand over my child's cradle.

I want to rock the cradle, but I'm afraid. My child's indistinct, tiny features crinkle in a grimace. Wind? Or plain misery? They say the bond between a mother and child is so preternatural they communicate telepathically. What vile, vicious thoughts am I bombarding her with? Or vice versa? *She* has invaded me. The doubt struck me like a blow even the very first time I saw her, the morning after she was born. The hospital nurse came into my room beaming and held her up.

'Take your beautiful baby,' she said, 'all yours.'

Why is she saying that, I thought. Is she really beautiful? This just-congealed, glutinous little clot of life that tore up my insides before slipping out to assert its being? Or is this another trick? Maybe she's not mine at all? Maybe they've got the tags mixed up and are trying to palm off someone else's baby on me. I accepted her from the nurse's arms reluctantly, with a gaping sense of disappointment.

I've been going through the motions. I spend my days and nights staring at her; when I'm feeding her, washing her bottom, rocking her to sleep, I stare at those thin lips, the tiny nose, the dazed half-closed eyes, the patches of rash she came with which haven't quite cleared yet, her all but bald, bumpy head, and I search my heart for feelings of love, of tenderness for this little creature swaddled in her baby clothes. There's nothing. I confess to it. Only numbness, a slight revulsion. I see no beauty here. Only my own annoyance and frustration and disbelief glaring back at me. I had thought that having a child would make my heart overflow with fountains of love; that this would happen most naturally, most effortlessly. It's not so. Instead, I am sometimes overcome by the most gruesomely sadistic impulses. It horrifies me that I can have such thoughts. But it does not move me to remorse or compassion, nor even pity for this child who has the misfortune to have a monster for her mother.

How unsuspecting, how utterly helpless and vulnerable she is. How easy to smother, to snuff out this little morsel of life. There have been times when, pacing the living-room floor with her senselessly yowling in my arms—indigestion, colic, the doctor said—when I have considered, no, that's not correct, the thought has crossed my mind of its own volition, how simple it would be to grip her by the legs and smash her soft skull against the wall. It's so easy to murder an infant. No one would suspect its mother, to start with. An infant could just fall out of its mother's arms by accident, and that would be that . . . I try, I do try not to think such thoughts, I try to summon up from some remote recess of my being, more human, more maternal feelings, but I come up with only a mute anger and a bewildering sense of betrayal, of having been the subject of a nasty practical joke.

Three weeks have passed since my body was cleaved in half, rent asunder, and it still aches. I could not take the pain. I thought I was dying. My spirit was crushed to a blubbering frightened mass of incomprehension. Your hips are narrow, the doctor said, and a first baby is always difficult. Breathe deep. Push. Push when I tell you to. I begged them to allow Ashok to be at my side. But it was against hospital regulations, they said. The nurses gloated, as if to say, well, lovemaking was fun—and now you have your just deserts! Might it have helped if Ashok had been with me? After all, it was he who wanted the baby so much. I wanted it too. I had hoped it would bring us closer, cement our love, give him something to be proud of me for—a beautiful baby. Instead, it seems to have taken him farther away from me.

He's so complete in himself, so self-assured. Where does he get his strength from? Not from me, that much I know. He lives in the real world. I am the neurotic one. The sad thing is, the baby seems to know it. The more I reject her in my heart, the more she cries and clings to me. She can go on suckling for hours on end, never willing to surrender my breast until sleep obliterates her will. I hate it, that squelchy unpleasant mooching which leaves my nipples sore. I wonder sometimes if this is not a battle we are engaged in, this little demon shrimp and I, if she's not some sort of succubus intent on draining the life out of me, entirely.

When suddenly the pain ceased, for an instant I felt a flood of joy, a great relief. I didn't even ask to see my baby, or want to hold her. I wanted only sleep. A long, lush, interminable sleep. The doctor obliged with a sedative as he put the final stitches on me. I was wheeled out of the labour room in a somnolent trance. And afterwards . . .

Afterwards, Ashok was jubilant. Friends and relations began

to pour in, pressing gooey, rich sweetmeats on me, books on babycare, clothes and gifts for Baby. Everyone was celebrating. Names were discussed. I made only one suggestion—Pia. It was immediately vetoed by my husband who said he once knew a real bitch of a woman by that name. In the evening, when the hospital gong sounded and everyone was ushered out, I was left alone with my baby, still thinking of her as Pia, and wondering who that bitch of a woman was and what my husband's relations with her were. Soon, even that didn't matter anymore, because by then the mindless unending routine which frantically cluttered up my brain—of nursing and burping, cleaning and bathing and minding Baby began. I was left with nothing: only resentment and a strange emptiness; the sense of having become a stranger to myself.

~

I glance at the clock on the wall. I still have an hour before the five o'clock feed. The watchman has already passed by twice again, tapping his stick louder than ever, no doubt still in a quandary about whether something is amiss at R-4 which requires him to act. R-4 is the number of our bungalow; one of my private nightmares is that I am lost, wandering randomly through the vast colony, ringing the doorbells of hostile strangers at the dead of night, and I cannot for the life of me remember our number . . . The watchman has stopped outside our gate. What does he want? Another glimpse of that woman at the window in a fog of yellow light? Shall I strip off my nightie and display to him this body of a beggar that hasn't been touched in ten months? I'm a beggar for love. I need help. My brain needs to sleep. The cats are quiet now, but soon another kind of wailing will assault my frayed, sleepless nerves. Sleep. Sleep while you can . . . I must have. When Baby's cries woke me up, for a few seconds I could not move. Even Ashok, a heavy sleeper, was roused and called out:

'Preeti . . . Preeti . . .! Baby's crying.'

Then the dream I had been dreaming came back to me, vividly electric. I had dreamt that Fuzzy was in my arms; soft, furry, unobtrusive Fuzzy. I was holding him to my breast and giving him suck. My teat was clamped between needle-sharp fangs. My whole being seemed to disintegrate, dissolve in a flood of molten lava that fused intense physical pleasure and overwhelming dread of sudden, searing pain.

Drowsily, I lifted Baby from the cradle and put her to my aching breast.

~

The next morning was blindingly white and dry. At breakfast, Ashok told me he would be leaving for Bhopal in the afternoon. He had to look at some premises and interview job applicants for the new branch they were opening there.

I kept my eyes averted and didn't say a word. Then he added, contritely, 'Can't help it . . . it's very important.'

'Must you go now?' My hands trembled as I poured the coffee, but inhaling sharply to dispel the tremor of helplessness in my voice, I yelled: 'There's a three-week-old baby in the house. Are you aware? How am I to manage alone? And why do you tell me *today*!'

'I had a word with Kanta when she came in the morning. You were resting,' he said, munching his toast calmly. 'She promises to be regular, at least while I'm away, and help you with the cooking.'

His composure was affected and unconvincing. He's scared, I thought to myself. He's afraid I'm about to create a scene.

'It's all very well-planned, isn't it,' I said coolly, now my turn to appear unruffled. 'Only I'm left in the dark. To sit at home and mind your baby.'

'Now, look, Preeti, it's not like that. What would have been the sense in my telling you days in advance, when I wasn't even sure I'd have to go. I just found out yesterday . . . I haven't had time. And it's only for two days, anyway.'

I counted the seconds silently. Then, after a significant pause, 'Who are you going with?'

I rapped out the question icily, at a measured pace. I can be quite a good actress when I'm feeling cornered.

That didn't sound so nice even to my own ears. It's not how I would have expressed myself, given half a chance. But with Ashok everything has to be measured and rational. Emotions must be curbed. Speech must be calculated and precise. My soul was crying to break down, weep bitterly, accuse him, grab his unblemished shirt and crumple it with my nails, and the flesh beneath as well. To confess to him what I have suspected for so long, what I believe to be true, what I long to hear him deny. *I want him to deny it if he can!* That he's been unfaithful to me. That he has used me to have his child. That from now on I have only a purely functional significance in his life.

'Alone, of course,' he answered with perfect nonchalance, and got up from the breakfast table.

In the afternoon, he came home again to pack a small travelling bag and have his lunch. The morning had flown by in an incredible mish-mash of disorder, loud crying and a general loss of control on my part. Baby wouldn't sleep and allow me time in the kitchen. When I tried to feed her a second time in the space of half an hour, hoping that would induce sleep, she brought everything up with a mighty heave and soaked me and herself in milky green vomit. I had to bathe and change her again, then wash myself while she lay bawling wretchedly in her crib. Just then Kanta walked in, half an hour late, and I lammed into her with such intemperate abuse that she blanched and offered to quit. For some reason I felt triumphant, as though I had won an argument. Quite unreasonably, I declared that I would be better off without her and settled her dues immediately, even making deductions for all the days of the month she hadn't come. This was madness, I knew. Or the beginning of it. I felt pretty gleeful about what I had done.

Half an hour later, Ashok walked in.

'Kanta has left,' I told him.

'What do you mean?'

'We had a row. She quit.'

'That's too bad,' he said quietly.

'You must postpone your trip, Ashok.' He didn't say anything. 'You can't go now. Please. How will I cope?'

'That's too bad,' he said again. 'If you wanted to quarrel with her, you should have waited two days.'

I didn't know whether to cry or attack him with my fists.

'So you will not give up your pleasure trip,' I spat out the words viciously. A muscle twitched involuntarily in my cheek.

'Have you gone mad?' he shouted angrily. 'I'm going on urgent office work, I've told you.'

'With that bitch?'

'What are you saying?' He looked genuinely aghast.

'With that bitch from your office whose name you have given to my daughter,' I screamed.

'Anjali . . .?' he stared at me open-mouthed. 'My God, Preeti, what's come over you?' He stepped forward as if he were about to take me in his arms and reassure me, then thought better of it and merely said, 'You've got it all wrong, believe me. The only relations I have with that girl are those of the workplace.'

'Then prove it to me. Don't go.'

'I know you are under a lot of stress, Preeti,' he said kindly, though patronizingly. 'So am I. I've got my work to worry about as well. We have our child's future to work for, together. How shall we, if we succumb to such mad delusions?'

'Don't go, Ashok,' I repeated dully. 'Please don't go. I beg you.'

He gave me a withering look of contempt. Then, without a word, he strode into our bedroom and started packing his bag.

His protestations were convincing. Maybe I am mad, maybe I am a fool not to trust his love. But I want him to put more effort into it, I want to torment him, break his defences. Why can't he share my suffering, I thought. If he loves me, why can't he sacrifice something for me?

At the door, just before he left I tried again, this time taking a different approach. I sobbed. I shed genuine tears.

'Forgive me, Ashok,' I pleaded. 'I'm sorry my filthy mind could accuse you of such things. But take pity on me. Just for today—don't go.'

'Look after yourself,' he said blandly. 'And Anju.'

Before he could shut the door in my face, I gave it a terrific shove which must have nearly knocked him down. Then I opened it again, and screamed hysterically at his receding figure, 'You have some hope . . .! Don't be too shocked if you come home and find us both missing. Or dead!'

It didn't work. He walked on down the drive at a perfectly measured pace, neither too hurried nor too slow, as though I were the impassive lens of a camera and he, a bored actor repeating the same shot for the nth time.

But I wasn't going to leave it at that. I noted the time he walked out with his overnight suitcase, and exactly an hour later, phoned his office. I asked the receptionist to connect me with Anjali Malhotra. I had met her only once when she came home with his other office colleagues to congratulate us on the birth of our child. I saw with my own eyes how much the two of them were drawn together, how they could barely restrain themselves from touching at the slightest pretext, if only a wrist or a shoulder. And that congratulatory handshake which seemed like it would never end . . . If she came on the line, I planned to disconnect without speaking. But no. She wasn't in the office, Miss Malhotra was on leave.

That was all I needed to hear. All it took to sever my already tenuous links with reality.

He's gone. My husband has gone . . . away.

~

What's today? Tuesday, Wednesday? I stare at the calendar, but the dates mean nothing to me. Is this the right month I'm looking at? Has someone been trying to confuse me by tearing pages off the calendar? The month is right, I think. Or is it? The dates dance before my eyes in their boxes, disdainfully. I am lost. I can't even remember what day this is.

Mind in disarray, everything's spinning. All around me, disorder blooms; sink overflowing with dirty vessels and plates. That can wait. I wander from room to room trying to decide where to start. I am looking for something, clearly . . . some indication or hint that will help me find my bearings . . . But what's this? A heap of old newspapers? Surely these will provide a clue? I get absorbed in reading the headlines. But no, it's not just the day date month or year I am searching for . . . It's the meaning of my mixed-up life I am looking for, of my soul, yellowed and tattered as this newsprint, and I hope to find it in these headlines? RAJIV GANDHI ASSASSINATED . . . TEMPLE AT ANY COST, SAYS ADVANI . . . GOLD RESERVES SOLD . . . EARTHQUAKE IN GARHWAL . . . Oh no, not this, none of this signifies anything . . . I begin ripping up the sheets, crumpling, twisting, shredding them, tossing them in the air . . . One more step . . . Just one more, and you'll have reached the point of no return . . . You can be free of the real world if you choose . . .

What is that most important thing which eludes me? I have a husband. He has gone away. But he did say he'll be back. That's it! When did he say? If only I knew . . . what day is today . . . It suddenly flashes on me I might feel better if I could only look at myself, gaze deeply into my eyes. Do I want that? I make a dash to the bathroom but can see nothing in the mirror. It's misted over. I wipe it with my hands. Then I hear the water flowing, and I remember I have left the geyser running for a bath. The tub is overflowing. How long has it been? And this? This heap of soiled nappies on the floor jars me back to reality long enough to hear a distant whimpering. My child! I had forgotten. I close the tap and rush to the bedroom. My child is crying so wretchedly she is gasping for air. I pick her up and put her to my breast.

I sit. Her rhythmic, gentle sucking relaxes me. My mind flowers with prurient fantasies. I see them enacted by two naked bodies. My husband's and that other woman's. I am angry and pained, but also feverishly excited by the spectacle. My body contorts with desire. So that's how it is. Someone else is having all the fun. I won't let him get away with this. How shall I punish him? Go out into the street and pick up the first handsome stranger I see? Bring him home and spread my legs for him? No, something more horrible, something that will make him want to tear out his heart in anguish and regret.

I know . . . I will wait till my child is asleep. Then go into the kitchen and, from the drawer, take the bread-knife. I'll creep up to her crib and, with all my might, plunge it into her tiny breast . . . Like Medea, the barbarian queen, who exacted such terrible vengeance for Jason's faithlessness the very heavens shuddered to witness it. What are those lines? 'Let none think me a weak one, feeble-spirited, A stay-at-home . . . It was not to be that you should scorn my love. My grief is gain when you cannot mock it.' My Eng. Lit. may stand me in good stead even after all these years. But I am not the stuff of Greek tragedy, don't I know it? I am weak, cowardly. And I don't know how to love . . . Oh, why did I have to give up everything? My studies, my poetry, my very imagination it would seem has withered. Why did I let everything go? I have become nothing . . . a mere shell, an empty pitcher thirsting for repletion. Oh fill me up, my man . . . my child . . . my God. Someone help, please.

What I went through in those two days! They could have been two weeks, two months; all notion of time had forsaken me except the most primitive, of darkness and light. I knew my mind was leading me onto very slippery terrain. It was a thin ledge I was walking, I knew, on one side of which lay many hardships, unpleasant truths about myself I didn't want to face, the stresses and strains of being alive; on the other, seductively poised, lay the freedom of giving up, of letting oneself slide into insanity. And every time I veered dangerously close to this other option, my child would yank me back to reality with her imperious howling.

Her crying was unbearable to my ears. I raged at her, screamed and shouted, held her up with both hands and shook her like a rattle. Why not just walk away from this hell-hole of unbidden and loathsome responsibility, I thought. I could forget to take the house keys, leave her in her piss and shit to perish from hunger and fever and thirst . . . But she did not give me that option, my little one was steadfast in her love. It was she who kept me sane.

Somehow when night came, both of us were completely exhausted, like predatory lovers after a day of frenzied copulation. We sank into a deep, wholesome sleep, and neither of us stirred till the gentle morning sun streamed in through the bedroom window.

~

I was still in bed when the doorbell rang. We had a visitor.

He was an old man of indeterminate age, short, wizened, but wiry. He was wearing a colourful patchwork jacket, and carried a satchel on his shoulder. When I opened the door he smiled, his eyes twinkling.

'I'm from the chemist's, madam,' he said.

My blank expression prompted him to elaborate.

'Jolly Chemist, across the road. Your order. I've brought it . . .'

'I made no order,' I said, hugging my housecoat close to my body, against the morning chill.

'But this is R-4 madam, no? You had phoned yesterday evening and placed an order. Here is your order form,' he said, not at all surprised by my disavowal. Maybe people did this all the time. Ordered things from the chemist and denied it later.

'What was it I had asked for?' I inquired with a mysterious feeling of trepidation. He handed me the order form. But before I could look at it, my child who had just woken up started crying inside.

'Oh, just a minute please, will you come in and wait?'

The old man smiled, looking pleased, as if this invitation was just what he had been waiting for. I was not afraid to let a stranger into the house. Somehow, I felt I could trust this man completely.

I brought Baby out, but she refused to stop crying.

'Oh please,' the old man said. 'The child is hungry. Please feed him. I can wait.'

I was not embarrassed. I threw a shawl over my shoulder, unbuttoned my dress and gave her my breast. The old man relaxed when the crying ceased.

'I have a daughter your age. She had a child just like him . . .'

'Her . . .' I corrected.

'Her name?'

'Anju.'

'Anju . . . She's a beautiful child. You must love her very much.'

'Your daughter . . . You said she *had* a child?'

'Yes . . . He died.'

'How?'

'It's a long story, and a sad one,' he said, his gentle eyes clouding with sorrow. 'Life treated them harshly. Her husband was unemployed. He couldn't find work though he tried very hard, that's the truth. Then he took to drinking. Somehow, in the delusion of his drunkenness and insecurity, he developed a conviction that his wife had taken a lover. That was the last straw for him. He decided to kill himself. And his wife and child. He brought home a box of poisoned sweets, saying that he had finally managed to find a job as a peon. He had to report for work in the morning. That night after dinner they all enjoyed the sweets. All except me. He didn't press me to have any, because they all know I am severely diabetic . . . The child was the first to die, within three hours, vomiting incessantly. He died later, in hospital. My daughter was the only one who survived that night.'

'How horrible,' I whispered, dazed and disturbed by the tale I had just heard, before I had time to even brush my teeth.

'My daughter blames herself now for everything. For nagging and tormenting her husband for his drunkenness, and their poverty. She has not been able to get over it yet . . .'

We sat there in silence for a while. I stared at the old man, who kept his eyes fixed on the floor. I could hardly believe that this early morning encounter was taking place. There was something unreal about it. About this old man in his colourful and shabby jacket, who had popped out of nowhere, like a character in a children's storybook. Yet, I was moved.

It was I who broke the silence.

'Will you have a cup of tea? I am going to make some for myself.'

'No, madam. Thank you . . . Er, those things you had asked for?'

Remembering, I looked at the list of things I was supposed to have ordered from the chemist. A roll of cotton, a bottle of Waterbury's Compound, some vitamin drops and a box of rat poison. Rat poison? Did I really ask for that? I shivered to think that in my madness of yesterday, I might well have. The day—it didn't seem like just one—had exploded into so many fragments, I wouldn't be surprised if bits of shrapnel embedded in unlikely places continued to surprise and sting me for years to come.

'Then you will not be needing these things?'

I hesitated.

'It's all right,' said the old man. 'There's no problem . . . The man at the counter who writes down phone orders often makes mistakes.' He stood, and picked up his satchel.

Again, I thought, this is too unreal. Am I still in bed dreaming?

'Wait,' I said, as he turned to leave. 'Who are you?'

'I told you,' he said. 'I am the shop assistant-cum-delivery boy at Jolly Chemist. Fact is, after all these years of working at a chemist's, I know a little about healing, myself. When it's a simple case, sometimes I even dispense medicine myself. Okay, madam . . .?'

I could have sworn there was laughter in his eyes, though his face was as deadpan as ever. I felt a deep surge of gratitude for this man who had by chance entered my life but a few minutes ago, yet, with a few simple words, had restored me, blessed my heart with unexpected grace. I was no longer beyond the pale, excommunicated from the heart of love, the source of all joy and being. I had been reprieved. I was about to stand up with Anju in my arms, but he motioned to me to remain seated.

As he stepped out of the front door and began to walk slowly down the driveway, I could hardly believe my eyes. A little distance away, at the gate to R-4, was a pretty black cat with white blotches, sitting daintily on her haunches. As the old man walked past her, she stood and followed nimbly at his heels. I was amazed. I know cats, but I have never before seen one that behaved so much like a puppy. He opened the garden gate. The cat followed him out, and they were gone. I never saw either of them again.

Anju had stopped suckling a while ago and fallen asleep in my arms. I shut the front door, then carried her into the bedroom and gently laid her in her cradle. With her eyes closed, her face relaxed in slumber, at last I saw her radiant beauty. A faint smile flickered momentarily on her lips. I glanced at the clock. She will sleep for another hour at least. When she wakes up again, I will be there at her side waiting, my breasts replete. I do not want her ever again to greet the world with that bitter, angry, voracious cry of wretchedness and despair.

Finely Chopped Dill

Jacintha was angry with the world for making her what she had become. In particular, it was a few individuals she held responsible. Sons of whores, daughters of bitches, may they sizzle in the hottest pit of hell. Tears stabbed and streamed from her eyes as she chopped a heap of deep purple onions.

She tried to silence the thoughts that were rushing to her brain, engorging it with a bitter rage. But they kept swirling back, dancing naked before her helpless distraction. Mocking her; not unlike the position of the hands in the timepiece on the wall which swam into vision every time she wiped her watering eyes. Already a quarter to one. A family of six would soon be hungry for chicken curry. Not counting the old woman in her backroom who would call for her soup and toast anytime now. Jacintha sliced faster.

By the time they finished with their meal and she could start on hers it would be at least a half past two, and all the best pieces consumed. Never mind, just so long as she could reach home safely. On days when lunch was ready early, they didn't mind if she ate first and came back in the evening to scrub the dishes. But today everything had got late. Perhaps it was best not to wait for them to finish licking their plates. Just go home to a fried egg instead. As she plunged the ground spices into hot oil, their aroma rose to her nostrils and her quandary became especially painful. She was very hungry herself.

She glanced at the clock again. Once it struck three, the street leading to the cluster of little cottages and shanties where she lived would be deserted. Shops downed their shutters in the afternoon. Apart from the stray autorickshaa hurtling past, everything was still as death. Two days ago, the same thing had happened. She was late. When she stepped out of Domasso Villa onto the hot tar of the street, there wasn't a stray dog, not even a crow in sight.

Then a white Fiat had pulled up at the pavement just a few feet away from her with four men inside. They looked this way and that, as if searching for somebody or something, but she could tell it was her they were really watching. She felt dizzy with fear. The men in the car were staring. She could feel their collective gaze boring a hole in the nape of her neck as she walked past. If one of them had opened a door and stepped out, she was prepared to make a run for it. But then, thank God, she heard the engine start up and the white Fiat rolled away. She sighed with relief, wiped the perspiration off her face and walked on.

She knew it was not her imagination. There were signs everywhere. Her movements were being observed. This was a new job, barely five months old. How had they found out where she was working? She'd avoided telling anyone about it, even her closest friend. But they were clever. Each time it was a different bunch of people, faces she had never seen before. So she wouldn't get suspicious. But she was no fool either. Once in a while, they slipped up, and she recognized among her watchers one of Cyril's boys from Fernandes Lane. It infuriated her that they could have the gall to subject her to such harassment. Sometimes at the paan shop she passed on her way home, a lone stranger would be hanging about ogling her shamelessly. She felt like stepping up and giving him two tight slaps across his face. But, she thought, better to pretend I don't see anything. Just keep walking on. Those bastards are capable of anything. If they could finish off a boy not yet twenty-three and dump his body in the pond, would they stop at harming a defenceless woman? Just because I know their secret, they're after me now.

Dolsy, the landlord's sister entered the kitchen.

'Muttering, muttering, what Jessie?' she observed kindly.

'What,' repeated Jacintha dully. 'Food is nearly ready.'

'Don't squeeze too much tamarind in the curry, baba,' purred Dolsy, her tone cautious and fawning. 'Poor Domasso's joints are aching so, dear.'

She knew she had to be careful how she put it. Jacintha didn't like her cooking criticized. There had been occasions in the past when she had absented herself for days over a slight rebuke about excess salt in the food or the pungency of a curry. And she wouldn't return until a peace effort was initiated—usually by Dolsy herself, much irritated but meek, dropping by to politely enquire after her health. Then Jacintha would come back to work, complaining of dizziness or her tortured varicose veins.

'I never put too much tamarind,' declared Jacintha, and Dolsy decided this was not the best moment to debate the issue. A little later, in a conciliatory tone, Jacintha added,

'I know. Sour things very bad for joints. My fingers ache every morning in water. But I eat. Raw mangoes 'pecially, can't resist. With little salt and chilli . . .'

Dolsy was all right. Not half so abrasive as Sylvie, Domasso's wife, who was alive when Jacintha had first started working here, eight years ago. Jacintha felt a guarded affection for Dolsy, who was unmarried, like herself. She didn't make it a point to stand by while Jacintha helped herself to her meals. Sylvie had watched like a hawk. But there were other things about Dolsy which irritated her. Why did she have to potter about the kitchen and pretend to help, sticking her nose into curries even before the aroma could come to a head?

Only once, Dolsy had dared to remark, 'That nice juicy breast I was saving for Domasso? Where it's gone?'

'What breast you're talking about?' she had replied in a hurt-filled voice. 'I took the neck. All bones.' Jacintha knew that she had told a lie, but her sense of outrage at the suggestion that she was not entitled to the best pieces convinced her that she was right to defend herself. She felt unlimited scorn for people who were miserly about food.

Food was all-important to Jacintha—and that it should be deliciously cooked. Before she had started doing it for a wage, cooking had given her more pleasure than any other activity in the lustreless routine of her life. A perfectly browned kabab or a hotly spiced curry that hit the palate at exactly the right pitch gave her a unique sense of contentment and equilibrium. She had seen better times when she could afford a leg of mutton at least once a week, and often enough other delicacies like tongue, or oxtail, or trotters. But her enemies could not stomach her happiness; those vicious people had destroyed it all in one fell swoop.

It had happened one night, more than ten years ago. The last of her customers had just left. She had turned off the light on the verandah and changed into her night-gown when the police raided her home. Hysterical, angry, confused, Jacintha had tried to physically restrain them as they carried away from her backyard her large canisters, her drum and the copper pots and pipe of her distilling machinery and loaded it into their jeep. She had lost control and scratched one of the policemen on his arm with her nails. He responded by lecherously squeezing her large breasts, and whispering something lewd to her. The memory of that touch still smarted and filled her with shame.

It was all part of a plan to humiliate her, deprive her of her livelihood. Didn't every other shack in her colony do a little side-business selling hooch? Then why had she been singled out? Why, if not out of malice on a tip-off by those scum who had her own blood in their veins? They had stood by and gloated as those rascals carried off her things . . . She had never been able to put together enough money to start her liquor business again. Instead, she began to cook for a living.

Jacintha was a gifted cook. Over the years, she had mastered traditional recipes, and even ferreted out those little secret touches which expert cooks are wont not to mention while describing the alchemy of their ingredients. She disliked the drudgery of cooking for others, and such large quantities at that, but she took pains over her job nevertheless. After all, she took her meals there as well.

But then, good as she was at her work, she was also

unpredictable. There were days when her mood was so spoilt, and that howling harpy she was forced to live with made it her mission to do just that, when she could come up with an angry concoction that tasted of nothing but red chilli, or some slop as bland as boiled cabbage. On such days she would not eat there herself. She would fast and spend the day remembering St. Andrew, her patron saint; or if she was too hungry, she would go home and beat up an omelette.

Every morning, the bitch would try and provoke her. Don't hang your smelly clothes to dry on my line. What an unbearable stink from the lavatory after you fart up the place. Your intestines must be rotting, m'n. What do you eat, men's balls . . .? What goes of yours what I do with my men, bitch? Why, you're burning with envy? It's my home, too, isn't it? You got married and came here. My father built it . . .

Usually, such ripostes ran on endlessly in Jacintha's mind the whole day long, but she managed to keep her mouth shut. Should she lose her reticence for even a minute, the harangue would quickly deteriorate into a slanging match that ended in fisticuffs and scratch-wounds. One morning, when Jacintha came to work, she displayed deep teeth-marks in a patch of blue flesh on her forearm. Her spectacles, which she held in her hand, had been snapped at the nose-bridge. Poor Dolsy was quite shocked.

'Now you know what kind of animals live in this village,' said Jacintha with a kind of gloating disgust, 'and what-all filth they're spreading about me.'

In fact, there were no men in Jacintha's life. There hadn't been for a long, long time. She slept on the mezzanine, where she kept a Primus stove and her few belongings in an iron trunk. Her brother Robert, his wife Bettina—the harpy—and their two grown children used the hall and bedroom and kitchen downstairs, and she did her best to keep out of their way. But there was only one toilet. And many unfortunate squabbles surrounded the use of this tiny cubicle, with its half-filled pail of water and the black orifice that ingested and evacuated the congealed poisons of a family's bodily refuse.

Sometimes, when Robert was sober, he would take up for his sister.

'Got a bamboo up your arse or what?' he'd expostulate with his wife, spraying with his insults a lot of spittle as well. 'Every morning you talk some idiotic rubbish.'

But those were rare occasions. Most mornings Robert was already quite drunk. If he was awake, he skulked in a corner of the hall beside the silent television set or under the altar next to it. Or, he would lie supine, muttering in a half-sleep endless imprecations directed against no one in particular. He was her blood brother. But did he care what became of her? They were all in it together. Part of a conspiracy hatched by Bettina, the whore, and that fiendish cousin of hers, Cyril.

Cyril was known as Elvis the Pelvis on Fernandes Lane. Swanky, debonair, profligate, he was either tinkering with his bike or revving up and down the cross-lanes of the settlement on it, when he wasn't flying. He was a purser with an airline. His lifestyle indicated, and popular opinion confirmed, that he had done well for himself bringing in gold biscuits from Dubai. There was another boy called Esveraldo, younger than Cyril, who had worked for the same airline. He had been found face down in the pond outside the village, dead. People said he had belonged to the same gang of smugglers. Esveraldo was the son of Jorem. Jorem had been engaged to Jacintha for eleven years before he decided to marry someone else.

She still saw Jorem sometimes, at funerals and weddings. Jacintha had accepted it as her destiny that she would remain a spinster. But spiteful tongues decreed that the reason why Jacintha never missed a funeral was because she was always hoping to glimpse her ex-boyfriend, or stand close behind him at the wake. This was sheer calumny. The truth was Jacintha was very particular, almost devout about observing her neighbourly duties. Her neighbours could depend on her in times of trouble, they were important to her. Of friends, she had very few.

There was one, Rosabel. But she had married and moved to Poisar. Years ago they had worked together in a biscuit factory. They had fallen in love, so close was their friendship. Rosabel's marriage and displacement had created a rift. But much tenderness remained and had reasserted itself once Rosabel discovered that the man she had married was selfish and violent. Still, sheer distance compelled their separation, and they hardly ever saw each other.

'If I told you all I know about the people of this village,' Jacintha always called the settlement where she lived a village, and that was what it was for her and many of its residents (she hardly ever crossed the railway tracks, let alone caught a train), 'your ears will burn with shame. And because I know so much they are after me now . . . I keep my mouth shut. Why to talk? Still they are not leaving me alone . . . my own family, they are the worst bastards . . . Won't stop to kill anyone.'

Because she spoke in riddles, Dolsy never quite knew what to make of Jacintha's outbursts, or what exactly it was she feared. She was eager to pick up the village gossip but wasn't sure how much of what she heard was Jacintha's own concoction. She felt sorry for this woman in her early fifties, still comely, though on the large side, who had to work so hard for a living, who was so alone and had so many tormentors. But she also wondered at times if everything was quite right in Jacintha's upper storey.

A few days later, something strange happened. Jacintha came to work dressed in the most unusual fashion. She was wearing a salwaar-kameez that was probably twenty years old, judging by the way it clung to her body. Instead of a dupatta, she had thrown a thin printed bedsheet over her shoulders and most of her face. Later on, Dolsy remarked on her behaviour to Domasso: 'What does she think, people are going to shoot her down in broad daylight? Four men got out of a jeep and one was carrying a gun, she says. She would not have been alive if the watchman of Hari Niwas hadn't stepped out just then. I told her, if you feel like that, just make a police complaint. Then let's see what anybody can do to you . . .'

Domasso disagreed. He scratched his white stubble and spoke dismissively in a nasal whine, 'I'm warning you, don't get involved. Tomorrow she'll go around telling everyone Dolsy told her to make a police complaint.' Domasso wasn't interested in Jacintha's problems. He had enough of his own just trying to collect rent from the likes of her brother and their neighbours who occupied his land. But Dolsy was concerned. Jacintha's anxieties had created some of her own—the thought of the domestic chaos that would ensue should her cook suddenly collapse.

Sure enough, Jacintha's work was affected. She began to absent herself more frequently and now her excuse was not her poor health.

'I felt too frightened to come, baba,' she said. 'Someone is always watching me. How to come? My last job also I had to leave because such kind of things started happening. Now they won't leave me alone . . .'

Her curries still turned out all right, but became more eccentric in taste. She rushed through her work, taking shortcuts she herself would have found appalling earlier. Dolsy overlooked a lot. She tried to dispel her cook's fears by logical argument. But Jacintha was convinced someone was trying to kill her. Where she had once displayed placid control as she contrived her culinary mixes, there was now a strange edge to her movements in the kitchen, the frenzy of a trapped creature. She'd even lost interest in eating heartily, which Dolsy saw as the worst sign of all.

For Jacintha there were signs of the danger that awaited her everywhere. The most innocuous of them (or at least what seemed innocuous to Dolsy) filled her with terror.

'When I go to sleep, every night I always leave my slippers carefully at the foot of my bed. Today I woke up, and they were gone. Then I found them at the other end of the room, soles upward . . . and my cupboard, I am sure I locked it last night, and put the key under my pillow. When I woke up it was open. And the key was in my handbag, which was in the cupboard. Are they opening my bags and cupboards also now?'

Then one day, on her day off, Jacintha decided to bake a cake for her young nieces, her brother's children. Perhaps instinctively she knew that this was an activity that would soothe her. When they were children they had been very close to her. Now they were at college and didn't have much time for their aunt. She carefully mixed the batter for a Madeira cake and left it in her old tin oven on the Primus.

When she returned from the market with fruit peel to decorate the cake, she was shocked to see it had turned black. No, it wasn't exactly charred, just coated with grime and sagging in places. The sight of the cake chilled Jacintha to the bone. She didn't dare to touch it. She let it lie in the oven all night. Something horrible had been done to that cake, she was sure. That night, lying in bed under the corrugated roof of her mezzanine, there were tears in her eyes as she watched the candle she had lit for St. Andrew sputter and burn itself out. Her own life was a bit like the cake, she thought. She wondered why it had not turned out golden brown instead of bitterly black. She thought of Jorem who had kept her waiting for eleven years and destroyed her youth. She could still forgive him, but it was no use. He had four grown sons, one of them now dead, and an obese wife.

Jacintha hadn't exactly witnessed the murder of Esvaraldo Gomes. But she had been able to imagine it exactly like it must have happened. When she heard that his body had been found in the pond, she knew who had done it. And they knew that she knew. These things are difficult to conceal . . . In a moment of sudden clarity, Jacintha thought, all this for property? They won't let me have a roof over my head in my own father's house? My room is what they are after, then let them take it. If I get a few thousands out of them, I'll go away. Maybe I can find a job somewhere with living quarters. A nice home, husband-wife both working, children to look after . . . But it has to be far away from here. Or they'll find me out again . . . They won't let me live. I know too many of their terrible secrets.

The next morning, Jacintha decided it wouldn't be right to let even the pi-dogs consume the poison cake, let alone her nieces. So instead of throwing it on the garbage heap, she stuffed it down the toilet. For some reason, the aborted cake blocked the gully trap and a number of buckets of water were required to flush it clean. There was a terrific row. Of course, Jacintha's intestines were blamed for the catastrophe, since nobody knew about the cake.

She didn't go to work the next day as well. When it was evening she decided to fry a mackerel for her dinner. On the way back from the fish bazaar, she nearly got run over by a speeding car. Jacintha thought she recognized the face of the driver. Her large body wouldn't stop trembling. It was some time before she could steady herself and walk home.

After that day of the near-accident, Jacintha disappeared. Nobody knew where she had gone. On the third day of her absence, Dolsy went to her place but her family claimed ignorance of her whereabouts. Bettina began to say something mean about her loafing habits, but Dolsy silenced her with a sharp look. Then Bettina said yes, they were all worried.

'They don't give a damn,' said Dolsy to Domasso, 'I could see that they were wishing she'd be found dead in a gutter somewhere.'

Dolsy wanted to inform the police that Jacintha was missing and tell them what she knew about her cook's fears—that someone was trying to harm her. But Domassso put his foot down most vehemently.

'Who do you think you are to poke your nose into other people's affairs? Mother Teresa? You want a cook, I'll get you a cook. I'll get you ten cooks. But we are not going to get involved with the police.'

Kind-hearted Dolsy began to wonder if she had not misjudged Jacintha. Perhaps her fears were not all imaginary. She might have come to a dreadful end after all.

~

Unable to bear the turbulence in her life anymore, Jacintha packed a small bag and left her house while it was still dark and caught the Virar fast to Poisar. She found the company of her friend Rosabel calming. The husband left them alone. In her small garden, Rosabel grew vegetables. She was especially proud of her lettuce and dill patches, which were of prize quality. Every night, she would cook Jacintha a hot lettuce soup, with a little finely chopped dill thrown in. It was an old remedy for nerves and insomnia. Here in Poisar, Jacintha could have slept as late as she liked but she would get up early out of habit, and listen to the birds. It was very quiet and lovely. She imagined that the birds were speaking to her, reminding her of long ago when she was a child, knocking down raw mangoes from a tree in her neighbour's garden. Her mother, too, used to grow dill in their backyard, she recalled. In fact, it was the taste of Rosabel's soup which took her back many years to the time when her mother was still alive.

Perhaps even more than the lettuce soup what really helped Jacintha was her meeting with Dr Rahim Ali Khan, a tantric medicine man and clairvoyant whom Rosabel consulted for all her emotional and physical problems. Dr Rahim received his patients in the small room of a seedy hotel in Poisar. The room was painted a garish green and decorated with tantric mandalas, and photographs of Dr Rahim's gurus. It was filled with the fumes of strong incense. When it was her turn, the fierce-looking, bearded doctor listened to Jacintha's troubles patiently. He counted her pulse, stared hard at her fingernails and asked her if she had been experiencing shooting pains in the left side of her body, to which Jacintha answered that she had. Then, taking out an amber stone as large as an egg from a drawer, he proceeded to gaze at it, and fell into a trance. After what might have been five minutes, he shook his head, rubbed his eyes and frowned.

Then he said to Jacintha, 'Yes, you were right. They have been trying to kill you. And you have had a narrow escape. But do not worry. They cannot harm you now that you have come to me. I will pray for your well-being day and night. You must wear this talisman always, which I am preparing for you. It will protect you.'

The talisman was going to cost more money than Jacintha had on her, and certainly more than she could afford, but Rosabel insisted on chipping in. The doctor turned away for a few minutes to prepare the little tin box which had a black string running through it. When it was ready, he tied it to her arm himself. Then Dr Rahim put his palm on Jacintha's forehead. It felt very warm. It slid slowly over her crinkled hair and came to rest on the nape of her neck, where its heat seemed particularly intense. He squeezed her neck and shook her gently. Then he murmured,

'Why you're worrying? I'm there . . .'

For the first time, Jacintha dared to look deep into his eyes. They were gleeful, laughing, a child's eyes. Her years of torment and suffering seemed to drop away, and Jacintha felt young again.

Whether it was the dill and lettuce soup or Dr Rahim Khan's talisman that proved efficacious, ten days later Jacintha reported back to work at Domasso Villa. She was peculiarly serene and composed. Dolsy scolded her for having disappeared, making everyone worry, but Jacintha only smiled with girlish shyness. In her heart Dolsy rejoiced at her recovery, and at the prospect of good meals once again. Then Jacintha went into the kitchen and prepared a gorgeously spicy beef chilli fry.

It smelt so good, Domasso's mother wanted to try some, instead of the clear soup which was all she could generally stomach. Jacintha was in her room feeding the bed-ridden woman for well over an hour. The greedy old woman wiped out a good portion of the dish. Then Jacintha went into the kitchen to eat herself.

Dolsy couldn't resist going into the old woman's room and asking her, 'What were you two talking about for so long?'

'Talking?'

Her mother-in-law couldn't remember. Then she said, 'Oh yes, Jessie was telling me about the birds. Every morning before dawn she would wake up and hear a koel singing . . . She was telling me how sweetly he sang, so sweetly . . . *Ooeeeooo, ooeeeooo* . . . That means the rains will be here soon.'

'Yes,' whispered Dolsy. 'And now that you've eaten so well, you'd better sleep, too.'

'Yes,' said the old woman, 'I think I will.'

It was only one o'clock by the time Jacintha had finished with her meal and scrubbed the dishes. Then she sauntered out of Domasso Villa perspiring profusely, visibly satiated by the mound of rice and hot chilli fry she had just consumed. She walked with light, dainty steps, her large fleshy body quivering, floating almost, on the wings of a mysterious fledgling peace.

Two Angry Men

I knocked; then pushed, and entered.

As usual, all was dark inside; but at the far end of the shadowy, carpeted chamber I could make out his enormous, shapeless body slumped behind an outsize desk. Whenever I cross the threshold of his plush cabin, I experience a moment of inexplicable consternation as though about to step into the cave of an enormous python.

'Come, Prashant, come on in. Let's see what we've come up with this time?'

He switched on a tiny spotlight whose yellow beam fell precisely on the paper I handed him; some of its light spilled onto the lacquered surface of the desk, the silver plaques that stood on it. His weak eyes, progressively deteriorating through adulthood, felt rested in darkness, so he claimed. Holding my copy almost to his nose, he glanced over it through thick, brownish lenses.

'Much better now, Prashant,' he said. 'Got a bit carried away with that last attempt, don't you think? We're selling high-fibre biscuits, man. Not manna!'

I seethed, but said nothing. It was he who had mooted the idea in the first place, that the product be promoted as a 'miracle' biscuit! I had only followed my brief.

'Not bad,' he repeated once again, patronizingly, 'not bad at all . . . Tell Subodh to take a printout of his artwork. Once I've added my

finishing touches, we can send it off to the client's for approval . . . maybe tomorrow itself . . . Oh, by the way, if you're through early, stop by in the evening, we'll have a drink.'

'This evening?' I mumbled, inaudibly.

'Won't be anyone else there. Just you and me . . . Old school buddies, recherchant du temps perdu . . . what say?' Then he made that soft, scratchy noise from the base of his throat, as if scraping up a gob of recalcitrant phlegm. I knew it well, and the sentiment behind it: amused, derisive, half-way between chortling and chafing.

~

The foyer was dimly-lit, deserted. The gurkha slouching on his wooden stool in the security cabin seemed fast asleep. He didn't stir when Ashutosh lumbered past; then stopped in his tracks, and cleared his throat loudly. Dead to the world. At eight-thirty p.m?

Ashutosh walked on to the elevator shaft, and pressed the button to summon the lift. It began to move with a whirring, and touched base with a distinct thud. This had the desired effect: the watchman woke up in confusion and stood abruptly, muttering,

'Salaam, saab.'

'So jaa, so jaa . . .'

The throwaway reply pretended conviviality, but couldn't blunt its edge of displeasure. What use is a watchman who sleeps at his post?

'Good night, raja. Bahut der ho gayee na, aaj . . .?' he muttered sarcastically, and slammed the lift door shut.

At the eleventh floor, Ashutosh stepped out, and sauntered down the passage. He stopped at a polished mahogany door with no name on it, and let himself in. Groping in the dark for a switch, immense relief flooded him as the living room lit up: not too brightly, though; concealed lights on dimmers; fiddling with knobs, he adjusted their glow to his liking.

It was a warm room, nevertheless. Every detail—colours, décor, furnishing—tasteful, uncluttered, designed by him. The tiredness he had felt, after an unusually long day at office, abated. No, there was no question of tiredness, he was home now. A bit winded, perhaps, that was all. Walking into the tiny kitchenette, he lifted the lids off two stainless steel degchis perched on the gas stove, peered and sniffed at their contents. Rajma and some leafies he couldn't identify, though both smelt appetizing. Another larger vessel at the side contained chicken curry and a hotpot beside it, chappatis. No rice? Ah, here's rice. The bai, who came in during the day, wasn't such a bad cook at all; what's more, she kept the place reasonably tidy. However, there was still time before dinner. Would Prashant show up, or duck, and make some excuse tomorrow?

A clear case of still waters running deep; just how deep he couldn't say, but slyly guarded and tentative for sure. Every time he received an invitation to party—and this evening couldn't be called that by any stretch of definition—Prashant could be relied on to raise a tiresome fuss; as though his weary reluctance to socialize barely just withstood the debauched insistence of his hosts. But wait, that was only the beginning.

Invariably, he would arrive late, looking exhausted, as though submitting to an overwhelming tedium against his own better judgment; then proceed to polish off half a bottle of his finest single malt with ease, while jabbering incessantly—some of the others would have served themselves by now and started eating—about the most inconsequential nonsense; then, late at night, stuff himself silly on whatever food remained in the serving dishes, wiping them clean—astonishing greed, or monstrous appetite, whichever it was, didn't portend well for the body's well-being.

No party tonight—he'd made that amply clear, just so Prashant couldn't make it a pretext for absenting himself. He'd better come: important matters had to be finalized. Yet, even as he considered them, he doubted if Prashant could be relied on to know what was good for him. An uncertain sort of fellow, always muddled when it came to knowing his desires and feelings. He glanced at his watch; even by Prashant's own standards of decorum it was rather late. He'd tried calling his cell, but had found it switched off. The doorbell would ring any minute now; or not at all.

Pulling an ice-tray out of his box-like mini-refrigerator, he dropped two cubes into a glass, and poured an inch of whisky over them. He left the whisky on the living-room table to chill, then went in to change into cooler casuals.

~

It's true, we were at school together. That's how I know him so well; even though here, in the office, he's my boss.

Eighteen years ago, he spent two years in Paris, taking expensive group lessons from the renowned Franco-Spanish artist, Bissot. Ever since, he doesn't miss a chance to roll his 'r's, or drop a phrase in French which nobody he's speaking to can understand. Believe me, that's the least obnoxious of his traits.

His dad, a wealthy stock-broker, could afford the luxury of Paris for his son at a time when the boy was obsessed with becoming a painter, an artist. On his return, the father even organized an exhibition of his work at a gallery in Bombay along the seafront. In the beginning, Ashutosh had shown some talent, decidedly. One or two of his first canvases had impressed critics for their 'astonishing originality'. But his dad died young, leaving outstanding debts. The family was in financial distress, and he decided to lend his artistic wizardry to an ad agency. Now he makes loads of money, and values his creature comforts somewhat higher than his art.

Overall, I suppose he conveys the impression of being a thoughtful, well-meaning and well-adjusted person, often lost in the intricacies of his own mental processes. Is this mere affectation of 'creative' self-absorption? In reality, I've found it could just as easily be something more down-to-earth, like turning over a nasty snub in his mind while waiting for an opportune moment to hit out at a colleague; or, as some of our staff have learned to their chagrin, plotting a malicious body-blow against some junior employee's career just when he was beginning to believe he had gained favour with the boss.

No one knows him better than I do. Under that veneer of intelligence and affability runs a really mean streak.

To start with, he deluded himself he would continue painting in his spare time; resign his post as Art Director once he was financially secure. But soon he was made boss, and Ashutosh couldn't find any time to paint; such talent as he might once have had deserted him ages ago. Now he says, when he retires from advertising—in five, or at most seven years he's sure—he'll take up his paintbrush and palette again. Such resolutions, conceived spasmodically in the seclusion of his mind, are reposed in the confidence of his old schoolmate.

Another self-deception Ashutosh has persisted with since our high school days—even then, he couldn't not have known how often I chose to avoid his company—is that we were always best friends. Even then, to bully and manipulate was second nature to him. His happiest year at school was probably the one during which he was appointed 'secret' monitor to the Art master. This dubious honour gave him Gestapo-like powers over the boys—to observe, note down and privately report names of students guilty of disrupting class etiquette during the latter's occasional absences from class. Upon his return, the teacher would subject the poor saps featuring on Ashutosh's secret list to varying degrees of punishment. In other words, authorized and incognito sneak, Ashutosh never hesitated to use his position to exact personal gain or revenge.

Oh, forget the past! Who cares? What's more pertinent to the story of the school friends is that this mythic closeness we're supposed to have shared has never to date vouchsafed for me any favour or special dispensation in the workplace; often not even the simple decency one might expect of a colleague. How I came to be working here is for me a distasteful story—too long to recount in any detail—but briefly, he enticed me with the offer of becoming chief of an independent branch in Pune or Bangalore. For three years now, nothing more has been heard of that.

I'm not complaining, though. To tell you the truth there's no other place in the world I'd rather be, at this time. I work in Mumbai directly under Ashutosh as his ace copywriter.

As I said, he's the boss. In the advertising firm he runs with an iron hand, his own position is impregnable. Blue-eyed boy of J. A. Abbas, scion of its doddering proprietor, who reportedly has one foot in the grave. Abbas drops in about once a month, and leaves everyday decisions about the company to Ashutosh—Ashutosh Khedekar, Creative Head, Perkins, Futehally and Barker. Perkins and Barker are based in New York. Ours is a prestigious and important advertising firm that's been prospering ever since it forged this alliance. Relatively small in size, but vying for No. 2 position, I'm told, among ad agencies in India—if calculated by net worth of clientele. We have another branch in Delhi. And, of course, the one in south India, on the drawing board for three years. When it comes to my own work, he does give me some independence.

What can I say? Never liked him much myself, and so far as I can tell, hardly anyone does: a selfish, obese and ambitious operator who hasn't taken the trouble to cultivate real friendships (probably that's why he clings to the idea of our presumptive school camaraderie). Most people who know him well—there's just a handful, really—regard him as pompous, self-obsessed and vain. In recent years, of course, many more have sought to ingratiate themselves with him—oh yes, flatter and cultivate and wheedle—once he had scaled so swiftly the stairway to success.

~

Lowering his bulk onto the sofa of his living room, Ashutosh raised the glass to his lips. Thoughtful, introspective . . . that's how he felt this evening. Some hard decisions had to be taken, though; maybe even some home truths spoken. But the first warming intake of alcohol brought an involuntary exhalation to his lips, relaxing his muscles. He felt distracted.

An inexplicable disquiet abraded his smug composure. This wasn't the first time it had cropped up—he was in a mood to address it—why do I feel like an intruder, every time I enter my own flat after dark—as though I were breaking in . . .? Ah, rubbish! Simply because my name plate isn't nailed on to the front door?

But I *wanted* it that way, so as not to crimp the classy *entrée* of my apartment with *bourgeois* conventionality. Just getting the interiors man to find a flawless plank of that imposing size—no knots, no joints—took weeks, literally . . . Anyway, all the watchmen in the building—even the postmen who visit it—all know who lives here!

It *was* his flat, there could hardly be any doubt about it. He'd used his own latchkey to enter. The spare key was with the bai who came in to cook and clean. He was a single man living alone, but he had bought the flat with his own money. And before she died, Ashutosh had paid his mother back every rupee of the amount he'd borrowed from her—after the builder who was re-developing the site of their old family bungalow at Dadar delivered a suitcase full of cash, and some cheques, besides, for the family to move out.

A portion of that money went towards buying this small but independent apartment. His mother, who was still alive then, moved in with her younger sister—a widow herself—in Sion. At first, she hadn't minded at all, nor for that matter, had her sister. Unfortunately, they began to squabble, and the arrangement didn't finally work out as pleasantly as they might have wished. During this period his poor mother became seriously ill. She didn't live long enough to assume possession of the new flat allotted them as promised—it took much longer to raise the high-rise than the builder had claimed it would—at the site of their demolished bungalow. That flat was locked up now, the keys in his custody.

His younger brother, Avinash, harboured some grouse about not having got a fair deal. But Avinash, his wife, his kids, were always welcome to use the place any time they came to Bombay. He had assured them of this repeatedly; yet his brother remained dissatisfied. When do we ever come there, he argued. It's only fair that the 'family flat'—that's how *he* liked to describe it—be transferred to his name, since Ashutosh, the elder brother, had already purchased another flat using family money. And, in the process, it was their poor mother who had had to 'pay a high price'.

Now that last bit was patently unkind, and intended to hurt. It had been an arrangement between Mother and him, and he had repaid the loan in full before she died. It was indeed sad that she had fallen ill while at her sister's, and had never recovered. Sad, too, that they had allowed the builder to bamboozle them into making a 'distress' sale at a time when the real estate market was at its lowest level in years. Some of the money the builder paid them came to Avinash eventually, as per his mother's stated wishes. But it wasn't just a question of money, he insisted; it's what she had to go through to make the independence Ashutosh was now enjoying possible—that was the disgrace.

According to Avinash, Aunt Madhu had resented her elder sister's moving in (not true! insisted Ashutosh to himself for the hundredth time). And later, having to play nurse through her illness, brought her sadistic impulses to the fore. She had been deliberately cruel. Such was Avinash's contention, but what was he basing it on? Ashutosh himself had never found any evidence of such cruelty or nastiness on Madhumita's part.

He had been to see his mother a number of times during her illness. He would have sensed it, had there been some tension between them. Mother would have indicated it to him. Aunt Madhu herself would have brought it up—at the time, all three of them were rather close friends. It would have been very unlike her to treat her elder sister badly, especially when she was ailing and dependent.

Well-settled in Bangalore, Avinash held a senior position in IT Solutions, the global computer software company. It was a job that came with its own three-bedroom apartment. His children were studying at a very fine school in the vicinity. Why should he, now, retrospectively, resent his elder brother's hard-earned success? He wasn't even saying that the flat be put in both their names—that might have been a reasonable compromise—he wanted it solely for himself! God, the greed some people were capable of . . .

The mid-town apartment Ashutosh lived in was in one of the older towers of the city built perhaps thirty years ago. Still sturdy, elegant and well-maintained, it was an enviable address to have. Neither too modern, nor too old-world; and conveniently located, given that in this city it literally took hours to get from point A to point B if you were travelling in a taxi or a private car. Usually Ashutosh preferred to walk to work, at around eleven o'clock in the morning. It took him only about fifteen minutes to get to his office. In the evening, though, he felt it unsafe to walk back—the broken pavements, unfilled trenches and open manholes Bombay's municipality had littered the streets with were literal booby traps for someone like him, with deficient vision—so he always hailed a cab (which cost him merely the minimum fare). But he was very glad for the morning's walk which gave him some exercise—he needed much more, of course, but for now this was the only fitness plan he could slip into his working day.

It wouldn't be incorrect, he felt, to describe himself as both self-made and successful. Ashutosh Khedekar was an artist. Well, an artist of sorts. He could have become a famous painter—world famous, even—had he pursued his talent more doggedly. As it is, as Creative Head of a well-known advertising agency, Perkins, Futehally and Barker, he had done quite well for himself. Those last two guys, Perkins and Barker, Ashutosh had met only once or twice when they visited Bombay from their Madison Ave. office, at the time of signing the alliance franchise with Futehally, the old man who was practically bedridden now. J. A. Abbas, his son, officially in charge of Bombay, was also general manager of the firm; but trusting Ashutosh implicitly, he didn't interfere in any executive or creative decisions.

As he stared at the large canvas on the wall, Ashutosh felt a deep yearning; but that was momentary. His allowed his mind to delve into his past achievement; through layer-upon-layer of intricately detailed visual evocation.

Multiple perspectives of a cityscape, in oils. High-rise buildings in the remote distance, surrounded by rows of tenement houses—a bird's eye view. In the middle of it all, a dusty courtyard, the scene of an animated game of cricket being played by excitable and bedraggled children. Was this centre-stage? Or the tumult of an impossibly snarled traffic junction, divided from the children's game by a broken strip of rusty metal paling? In the foreground, a tall chimney spewed black fumes. A disorderly queue of workers waited patiently before an ornamental wrought-iron gate they would presently enter at shift change. The gate, entirely disproportionate in size to the workers clustered below, loomed menacingly large over them, and the entire distorted diorama.

He knew the painting well. He had spent weeks perfecting it, and could still devote hours to gazing at its abundant detail, which allowed the clashing perspectives and rudely contrasting dimensions to blend into a swirling, dizzying, composite whole. Six by five, the whole canvas was a multi-dimensional, variegated *tour de force*, dominated by greys, ochre and brown; he had named it 'Bombay, My Chaos'. Proud of the painting, as of the title he had given it, he decided against putting it up for sale. Many others had gone, quite a few canvases and watercolours, but this one he had decided to retain for himself.

In those early days, when he came home from France, international interest in Indian art was still very lukewarm. Yet, he knew he could have made it to the top—he was pretty sure of that even now—regret, if there was any, was only about not pushing himself hard enough. It would have meant a period of struggle, of roughing it out. Instead, he had allowed Papa's untimely death to decide matters for him; he had assumed responsibility for his family. Avinash had still not finished his college education when Papa died; among other things, he provided for his fees, saw him through university. And now, that same brother was eyeing a bigger portion of *his* pie.

Expecting Prashant he may have been—and for quite some time, too—but so intimately had his mind penetrated the interstices of the painting that the soft chimes of the doorbell, when they came, stabbed his consciousness with startling ferocity; it took him a moment to collect himself, rise from the sofa and amble to the door.

~

When Ashutosh says he wants a drink—just him and me, for old times' sake—it makes me want to laugh. Does he want to dig up dirt on some staffer? Or simply fling seeds of gossip in my backyard, hoping they'll catch and flourish in the quagmire that's PFB, Bombay . . . A tricky and devious character is our Ashutosh, my old school friend . . . Better keep an excuse ready: he'll be peeved I'm turning up so late . . . What's taking him so long to answer?

'Hi, Prashant,' Ashutosh greeted him, swinging the solid mahogany door wide open, just as Prashant raised his arm to ring again.

'Come on in. Glad you could make it . . . Sit, sit. Do sit. Pour yourself a drink,' he said, lazily indicating the tray holding a nearly empty bottle of whisky, a glass and an ice-bucket. 'There's soda in the fridge . . .'

Ashutosh flopped onto the large, soft sofa he had only just climbed out of, without waiting for Prashant to find a seat.

'I will, I will, boss, thanks,' said Prashant settling on the edge of a single-seater, 'no hurry. I'll help myself . . . I do know my way around.'

'You'd better, you bum' said Ashutosh. 'All those years of hanging out together . . .' They laughed. 'But why so bloody late, man? I'm already starting to feel hungry.'

'Sorry, Ash. Got held up at office just after you left.'

In using the abbreviation of Ashutosh's name, that harked back to their student days, Prashant was hoping to mollify the boss; but the ploy didn't seem to be working.

'Oh, did you?' retorted Ashutosh, voice dripping with irony and disbelief. '*I* imagined you were up to your old tricks again.'

'What old tricks?' countered Prashant coldly.

'I mean, you know—like slinking out of social engagements, while everyone else keeps waiting for you to arrive—like you've done so often in the past . . .'

'Everyone else? You told me you weren't expecting anyone else . . .'

'I know, I know . . . Just speaking generally. Of other times.'

'Nothing of that sort. Subodh had a problem sizing the artwork . . . I had to help.' Prashant explained, rather earnestly. 'And just when we had got it right, the colour cartridge ran dry. He ran down himself and got us a new one.'

Does he take me for an idiot? He was probably holed up for a couple of hours with the receptionist in one of Kit Kat's private rooms, over coffee and chicken sandwiches. It's scandalous, the way he's paying court to that little slip of a girl!

'On credit, I suppose?'

He doesn't believe me. What right does he have not to, to disbelieve what I'm saying to my face?

'I suppose so. The new stationery shop maintains a monthly account, I believe, of all PFB purchases.'

'But where the hell was that idler, Nandu?'

Ah, this isn't going right . . .

'Nandu left early. He asked me if he could go; a wedding in

the family, I think he said . . . It was the receptionist who stayed back and locked up.'

'H'm . . . Pinki . . . Pretty girl . . . good-natured, too, willing to do anything you ask her . . . She's still on probation, though. Well, I do wonder sometimes, what's with this other guy.'

'Which other guy?'

'Why on earth would a layout artist have to rely on a copywriter to execute a print-out?'

'For heaven's sake, Ash, it's just that Subodh's unfamiliar with the new software which, if you remember, we had installed only last week. I've used it before. So I was able to help him.'

Maybe it wasn't fair to use Subodh as my alibi . . . This asshole can become unreasonably vindictive when he chooses to. Stores away information, God knows where, then pulls it out when it suits his purpose. Why don't you mind your own business, fucker? What's it to you anyway? I should have told you outright I've a date with Pinki, can't make it to your bloody old school nostalgia evening.

'What's a guy like that doing in our firm, I ask myself. We need fully trained and capable people.'

'Oh, he'll pick it up soon enough. It's no big deal . . . Subodh's good at his work otherwise, wouldn't you say? Now don't—'

A silence followed: Prashant hadn't completed his sentence, and Ashutosh wasn't listening anyway. Rolling his powerful jowls, he masticated a mouthful of cashews thoroughly; then remembering Prashant, pushed the bowl in his direction.

It's disquieting, thought Prashant, selecting a cashew; *he could be staring at you and you wouldn't know it: there's no meeting of the eyes.* His purblind gaze made Prashant feel uncomfortable, somehow guilty, too.

But in that very moment, his mind had wandered away, back-flipping distractedly to Kit Kat, two hours ago . . . Pinki had found the shreds of chicken in her sandwich smelly; the bread, visibly dry, was falling apart. The waiter's incredulous, open-mouthed expression had stuck in Prashant's mind like a cinematic 'freeze'—was he being deliberately insolent? Instead of taking away the plate of sandwiches, as Pinki had asked him to, he merely stared at her like an imbecile for perhaps five whole seconds, not even lifting it off the table. Until *he* repeated her request more firmly. Or could it be he was just very surprised to hear her complain, since none of the couples who occupied the half-dozen or so semi-private cabins with a bi-partitioned swivel door—as he and Pinki had been this evening—ever cared to remark on, or even notice the quality of food served them?

Frankly, he couldn't detect any offensive odour in the chicken himself. But then he assumed Pinki's olfactories, more pristine and unspoilt than his, could identify odours more sensitively . . . All those years of unbridled smoking would have taken their toll, he was trying to curb the habit now; she was terribly put off by the smell of tobacco and smoke, and promised to help him stop . . . *Ah yes, how awful to tear himself away from Pinki—just to keep a date with Ashutosh? Never mind that he'd got here so late, even now he couldn't stop reproaching himself for not bringing her along although she had refused flatly, saying she wouldn't feel comfortable turning up uninvited to the boss's dinner; which, in any case, he had intended as a tete-a-tete between two school friends* . . . But Prashant became increasingly restless as the evening progressed, his mind running up obsessively against a recurring lament: how much more enjoyable the evening could have been, had she been here with them.

'What?' asked Ashutosh.

Prashant didn't get it.

'Now don't—what?' he repeated. It took Prashant a moment to recoup the thread of their interrupted exchange.

'Well, I was just going to say—don't go making any abrupt decisions about your staff.'

'And why not, may I ask? Do you mean I should let sleeping dogs lie . . .?'

'Just what the fuck're you trying to say, man? Why don't you speak more clearly?'

So irritable and uncontrolled was his reaction to Ashutosh's observation that the moment he blurted it out, his breath caught in dismay. For one befuddled moment he had imagined Ashutosh was calling him and Pinki sleeping dogs and liars. Anger shrivelled to chagrin; he realized he was gulping his drink down too fast. Covering up nimbly, though, he continued in a very reasonable voice, 'No, really, you're getting it all wrong, Ash . . . believe me, Subodh's a good kid.'

Not taken in by the sudden change of tenor, Ashutosh continued to chortle and leer at him in his uniquely reptilian fashion . . .

Jokes and gossip about his relationship with Pinki were rife in the office, Prashant could hardly expect Ashutosh not to have encountered any of those. Their age difference was striking, for one thing: Prashant was practically middle-aged, and Pinki, barely twenty-three. To make matters worse, somehow the staff had got wind of the fact that his wife was expecting their first baby in three months.

The truth was there was no physical intimacy between Prashant and Pinki, not even during those spells of monopolizing Kit Kat's private cabins. Sometimes, when secluded thus from public scrutiny, she allowed him to hold her hand; but for a few minutes or seconds only, before gently disengaging it from his grasp.

Shy, and evidently lonely, Pinki hadn't found it easy to make friends in the office. Somehow, she had been drawn to Prashant, or perhaps merely felt obliged to accept his first invitation to join him for a coffee after work.

'You are like my elder brother, sir,' she had said to him on that same evening, as though 'legitimizing' their first outing together.

'Please call me Prashant. I feel old enough as it is,' he had said.

She laughed; she was fascinated by him, he could tell, even a little overawed. He did most of the talking when they were together; she listened, and he felt protective towards her. During their now frequent after-office evenings together, he had come to know very gradually, of a deep sorrow in her heart. Her father was an alcoholic, and something of a sexual pervert, too, who picked up young boys and brought them home with him; her mother was silent and long-suffering. This much he had gathered, though she never wanted to speak further of family problems if she could help it.

His own feelings towards Pinki weren't so noble or fraternal, he had to admit; even though he saw the situation for what it was: impossible. She was young enough to be his daughter; yet he could barely resist imagining her youthful body against his own. He didn't enjoy fantasizing about it, even so . . . to lie in bed beside her would be to take part in a miracle of life, he couldn't deny it; it would be to shed in one amazing instant all those years of accumulated tiredness; to recapture in one embrace lost youth. When he was Pinki's age himself, he was attracted only to older women, believing that only a more mature woman would understand the complexity of his soul.

Now the woman he had married was about the same age as he, and she had become pregnant practically on their wedding night, even before he had had a chance to get to know her. He couldn't relate to her, not in the same magical way that he could to Pinki. But, apart from all that, he wasn't oblivious of the abnormality of his obsession. Many evenings later, when he had tried in various oblique ways to indicate to Pinki how much she meant to him, it was as if she had anticipated and understood the swell of romantic feeling in him. What she said to him, mature beyond her years, was right on; she appeared to have seen through his moribund self-deception very clearly.

'You're fooling yourself, Prashant . . . It's only an illusion. There's nothing I have to offer you. The day we decide to try—God forbid—to live according to the promptings of your fantasy, the spell will lift. It will vanish like a daydream, believe me . . .'

Then, interrupting his friend's reverie, with glazed eyes and a wide smile, the boss raised his glass in Prashant's direction.

'Okay, I say! So no more talking shop this evening . . . Are we agreed on that? I'll say bottoms up!'

Never one to drink slow, Prashant knocked back his half glass of whisky and soda, and offered to refill.

'Go ahead, pour it all in,' said Ashutosh, referring to the two inches of whisky remaining in the bottle. 'I have another one in the bar cabinet.'

'Oh good,' said Prashant, draining the last of the amber liquid into their glasses.

Both men drank a great deal; they conversed, laughed, gossiped, shared reminiscences of schooldays, laughed again. Pleasantly high, and enjoying themselves, apropos of nothing Prashant asked his friend if he'd heard about the passing of Fr. Aguiar? After a long and mysterious illness, and a prolonged hospitalization, their old school Principal had finally died. Ashutosh said he hadn't heard, but presently struck an even more sombre note.

'What are we talking about? I heard something even more terrible just this morning—I should have remembered to tell you right away,' he said. 'C'est incroyable . . . Quelle mauvaise chance . . . And my news is much more immediate: Chris!'

'What?'

'Chris! Don't you remember Chris De Mello?'

Prashant stared blankly.

'You've met him at least twice at our parties . . .'

Oh. You mean head honcho of Trimurti?'

'That's right. Only, he's not likely to be head of anything for some time now. Chris had his second major heart attack last night and was shipped to the ICU. Surgeons are planning an emergency by-pass on him tomorrow . . . Poor guy. What things happen to people, really . . . So brilliant! He was the brains behind TAP: all those highly successful campaigns they did in the nineties? Titan watches . . . Woodland shoes . . .

TBZ . . . Govardhan Ghee . . . He was responsible for all of those. Known as whizz kid from the time he joined Lintas, fresh out of college. Within three years, he had set up his own agency, Trimurti Advertising and Publicity, and within three or four more, TAP had topped the charts. He's not much older than either of us, you know, but what a brilliant career; the stuff of legends. It's he really who made Trimurti India's number one . . .'

'You sound like you're writing his obituary . . . Chris hasn't popped it yet, you know.'

'No, of course not, I wish him the very best . . . But something like this happens, and a man will never be quite himself again. I'm so sorry for poor Chris . . . To make matters worse,' he added as an afterthought, 'he was an excessive smoker, you see. One of his lungs has collapsed as well.'

Maybe you'll say I'm being unfair, but whenever Ash wears his mantle of compassion it makes me want to sneer. Sure enough, a minute or two later, entirely unmindful of its implications, he revealed the subterranean source of his merciful effusions.

'The only mistake Chris made was not to groom a second line of command, someone who could continue his good work in the event of a disaster like the one that has just occurred . . . It's not possible to make predictions like these, of course, but I'm pretty sure from now on TAP can only head downhill . . . A real pity, honestly.'

'Not if PFB can take their place as number one . . .'

'That's always a possibility, of course, but hardly something we should be debating now, with poor Chris lying in a hospital bed . . .'

He says that so reproachfully, in such a pained voice, I feel immediately guilty; but then on reflection, wonder: can an individual be so insecure about his own position in life, yet so egotistical as to want to second-guess the life spans of his competitors? I've noticed this before, too; he's the only person I know who seems to take a secret pleasure in others' afflictions, prognosticating as it were on their behalf, 'Poor sucker . . . he's not long for this world. A few more months, a year or at most two, then he's gone. I'm still young and healthy, thank God. I have at least twenty, twenty-five years ahead of me . . .! Not in exactly those words, of course, and not aloud, but—I do know my school buddy quite intimately, don't you think?

'Well, right now there's nothing we can do for Chris anyway, Prashant . . . But tell me, then, how's Prema doing?'

That's nothing short of calculated ambush. Prema is my wife, and she's six months pregnant. He throws the question at me with deliberate nonchalance, but his tone of voice, and what immediately preceded his question—my dig about writing Chris's obituary—the timing of it—convinces me it reeks of pure malice. Still, I keep my cool . . .

'She's doing fine, I guess, next week starts her seventh month, and then she'll move to her parents' until after her delivery; maybe even stay on a month or two after baby is born . . .'

About a year ago, Prashant had submitted to an arranged marriage, at his parents' bidding. They had found for him an orthodox Maharashtrian woman belonging to their own caste, somehow overlooked by the marriage mart. She was almost as old as Prashant himself. Even at the time—when he came to office carrying a printed wedding invitation for him—Ashutosh had expressed concern, asking Prashant if he knew what he was doing. While they were at school together, Prashant was always getting himself into the most awkward predicaments simply because he wasn't willing to speak his mind. And now the new bride was already pregnant, and heading towards delivery; about two weeks ago Prashant had asked for leave to be able to accompany her to the gynaecologist's.

Ashutosh had first heard rumours about a liaison between Prashant and the receptionist a month ago. Someone in the office had remarked on it rather enviously. Discounting it as no more than gossip, believing marriage should have sobered his friend, he had refused to take the rumour seriously. Until he saw them himself, huddled behind a table and coffee cups at a cafe not far from office. Pinki, who *was* very pretty and sexy, had been with them only two months, and had instantly becoming the cynosure of all eligible eyes. And some ineligible ones, too. Such as that damn fool, Prashant's . . . Couldn't he see he was being recklessly irresponsible? He could end up causing a lot of pain all around.

'Then the timing couldn't be more perfect . . .'

'For what?'

'Next week, I want you to take a flight to Bangalore. The interiors of our new branch are almost done; recruiting will start soon. Shantanu's been supervising everything until now, but I've let him know you're going to head Bangalore. I want you to be fully involved with interviewing and hiring the team. I trust your judgement completely.'

'So it's finally come through . . .'

'Sorry it took so long, Prashant, but these things usually do . . . When you agreed to join PFB, if you remember I had said you would head Bangalore . . . I like to keep my promises . . .'

'But the timing couldn't be worse!' Prashant protested. 'I'm married now, and my child is due in three months. I can't leave Prema here—'

'No, of course not, I see that. But she'll be with her parents these three months, won't she? And during this trip, I want you also to look out for an apartment that you think will suit Prema and you and the much-awaited addition to your family. PFB will pick up the tab. Just find it for us . . . A 3 BHK . . . anything up to forty or fifty lakhs. You know my brother, Avinash, of course? He'll be able to guide you on real estate . . . Something not too far from office. What do you say . . .? Can I ask Ruby to book your ticket? And for now, a room at a nice three-star hotel like Blossoms or First Residency? Before you leave, remind me though—I'll have some gifts I want you to carry for Avinash. And as for helping to recruit the staff—I don't need to say this—there'll be a bonus in it for you as well. I really think you'll like Bangalore . . . Don't forget, once we've cornered the southern market, it's only a matter of time before PHB is number one.'

'But I can't go now—'

'Ah, Prashant, I feared you might have objections. Don't tell me you've become attached to the attractions of our PFB, Bombay—'

'It's not that . . .'

'Pinki's a lovely girl, I won't deny it . . . but you're a married man now, you have a baby coming soon . . . You're completely gaga, mon ami to behave like this. Like a teenaged kid.'

'What the hell, Ash? Don't say that. Pinki's just a friend.'

'And so are we, I hope, you and I . . . You shouldn't turn

grumpy just because I say a few things plainly to you. I am older than you after all, you're behaving like a foolish teenager.'

'Only by a year and three months, isn't it?'

'Whatever. But I care for you as I would for a younger brother . . . You made a choice when you got married. Now you're not even giving it a chance.'

'I told you,' Prashant almost yelled back, 'Pinki and me—we're just friends!'

'Then a three-month—or two-and-a-half month—separation shouldn't pose such a problem?'

'Somehow I get the feeling, boss, you're making me an offer I can't refuse . . .'

'You really shouldn't even try to.'

~

As it turned out, Prashant spent a rather nice two months in Bangalore. The weather was lovely, and he quite liked what he saw of the city. He already knew Shantanu a little from the latter's time at PFB, Bombay, and found him very comfortable to work with. They drank together frequently after work at a nearby pub; and, on two occasions, at his home, when Shantanu's wife had prepared dinner for him.

The interviews went well, and most of the time they found themselves in complete agreement about the choice of candidates.

Frequently, during these two months, he thought about his own life. About Prema, whom he telephoned at least once or twice a week; about Pinki, whom he phoned less often; and a great deal about his friend, Ashutosh. Away from the office and his despotic ways, he began to wonder if he hadn't judged him too harshly.

He had kept his word about the Bangalore position, hadn't he, and been quite generous in the bargain, too? For three years, Prashant had chosen to believe it was only a ploy, a carrot he had dangled before him at a time when he was trying to persuade him to join his firm. Quite frankly, he was willing to admit he could have been wrong about many other judgements he had made about Ash. That particularly cruel observation spelled out silently to himself during their last evening together—just one example—about Ashutosh's vulturous gloating over the sick and dying—did him little credit.

In fact, later he had felt quite ashamed to have thought so. A more compassionate understanding had occurred to him: that such behavior, if it was at all true, must have its basis in Ash's own insecurity, his private disappointment about having sacrificed his talent at the altar of commerce, and the knowledge that time was running out for him, just as quickly as it was for others . . . No matter how much he pretended he would return to painting after retirement, he probably knew he would never be able to reclaim the gifts he had so casually frittered away.

And what about my own frustrations, thought Prashant? Occasionally, during those inebriated evenings he spent with Shantanu at the pub, his mind wandered off to his last year at school. One particular memory was indelibly etched in his subconscious—he had been unable to forget it . . . Students were busy swotting for the finals, brooding over prospective colleges and careers. Standing outside their school canteen,

Ashutosh was telling him that his father had decided to send him to Paris to study art. He could never forget the moment of intense envy and rage he had felt, about the unfairness of it all. During their school years, he had in fact himself fancied his own skills at drawing and painting; Ash, by common consensus, was considered the superior of the two. When he finally took a decision about his career, Prashant chose to enroll in a school for journalism. He had more than one talent; he was something of a writer, too. Yet, after much ado and exertion as roving reporter, and later as sub-editor of a tabloid newspaper, he had decided to try his hand at copywriting; it paid better even though in his opinion it was certainly the tritest form of writing.

And now, this fatuous obsession with a girl half his age? Wasn't *that* about trying to impede the slow drift towards old age and, eventually, death? What elixir of youth was he trying to imbibe by devouring that child sexually? Even if he never dared enact his fantasy, wasn't that the tune playing in his mind all the time? What gave him the right to be so critical of Ash's own failings and foibles? Oddly enough, now that geographical distance separated him from Pinki, he hardly ever thought of her. In fact, more often, he would wonder about how Prema was getting on. He must phone her again, soon.

Towards the end of his Bangalore sojourn, a curious thing happened. Every time he tried calling Pinki on her cell phone, he would find it switched off. On one or two occasions, it even rang, but was immediately interrupted by a recorded message saying that the user he was trying to contact was busy. When he dialled once again a few minutes later, he found it 'switched off'. The only explanation he could imagine was that she had lost her phone—or it had been stolen from her—and the thief had changed the SIM. But, if that was indeed the case, she should have phoned him—she knew his number—at the very least. For a few days he resisted calling the office exchange and asking for Pinki, since that would, he thought, certainly fuel further rumours in the office about their friendship. Then, a few days before he returned to Bombay, he called the office and asked for her but was told by the operator that she was no longer working there.

Prashant was puzzled. The fact that she had left no forwarding address or phone number was even more inexplicable. But soon, he had much else to occupy his mind. Prema phoned that night to say she had had a sensation of cramps coming on the previous morning, and had made an emergency visit to her doctor. It proved a false alarm, but after examining her, he did suggest that her husband should consider returning home as soon as he could, if he wanted to be present at the time of delivery. The baby might arrive sooner than they had anticipated, he said. The very next morning, Prashant booked a flight back to Bombay. Anyway, his immediate work at Bangalore was done.

~

After a whole day spent discussing work-related matters, Prashant couldn't resist asking Ashutosh about Pinki, why had she quit?

'I can't remember what she said,' answered Ashutosh, 'or if she even gave a reason. Maybe she found a better job . . .'

But Prashant wasn't convinced, and pressed Ashutosh further.

'I really don't know,' he said. 'You could try asking her girlfriends in the office why she didn't leave a forwarding number or address . . .'

'She never had too many friends among the female staff . . .' said Prashant.

There was something about what Ashutosh was saying that didn't convince him; even his manner seemed evasive.

A horrible thought occurred to him. *There's certainly more to this than meets the eye.* He began to feel angry with Ashutosh. *Could the bastard have used his power over her job to pile on to her, believing Pinki to be licentious, 'available'? That might explain why she felt so disgusted as to not even want to contact him—he was the boss's old school friend, after all—to tell him she was leaving.*

What Ashutosh said next to Prashant, reinforced his suspicions; to the point where he began to feel almost queasy at the thought of this fat frog pawing, intimidating the delicate Pinki . . .

'Well, you can't have everything in life, can you?' he said. 'You're a lucky man, Prashant. You have a pretty wife, a bonny baby—any day now, a promotion to branch manager, and a fabulous office flat to top it all. You shouldn't regret the minor collateral loss of a receptionist . . .'

It was just too much for Prashant to take. He lost control, and yelled, 'You bastard! I *told* you we were just friends!'

But Ashutosh wasn't fazed by abuse. He merely chortled, producing that soft snigger in his throat that Prashant knew so well, and said:

'Que plus dommage . . . Anyway, since she did do the skip on you while you were away on official work, I hope you'll feel sufficiently compensated by—'

And he held out a bulky bundle of 500-rupee notes.

'. . . your bonus, Prashant, for a job well done.'

Prashant took hold of the bundle of notes, feeling nothing but a deep hatred for his friend; he nodded a few times, stiffly, then said with deep sarcasm,

'Well, you're the boss, Ash . . .'

Late for Dinner

Fardoonji folded the morning's issue of *Jame* neatly and placed it on the glass-topped teapoy next to him. The light in the room was poor. From under the speckled and scarred glass, his ancestors peered dimly at him. Arranged at diagonal angles in a pattern which ran along the teapoy's border, they were faded and yellowed with age. Cawasmama, Ardeshir, Sorabji, all there, in their long duglees and prayer caps: as though time had been playing tricks with their faces, the thick layer of mustiness which had collected on the inner surface of the glass further distorted the images below. Tomorrow I must take a piece of mulmul and wipe the glass clean with spirit, thought Fardoonji, as he lowered his right leg from the easy chair, slipping his foot into the moist warmth of his rubber sapaat. The left leg he allowed to remain where it was, extended on the wooden leg-rest; that was the one that ached him at the knee.

From outside came the sound of a door being bolted and locked. That must be the Gorimars, the new young couple next door. Then half-blind old Aimai would be alone tonight. They shouldn't leave her this way, all alone; already one foot in the grave, who knows when her time may come? Fardoon glanced at the large pendulum clock on the wall across. Nine thirty. They'll never make it in time if they are on their way to the theatre, or to a movie. But perhaps it's just a party they're going to, a gathering of friends. Fardoon took off his spectacles and rubbed the bridge of his nose gently; then he looked at his wife, Sheramai. Sitting opposite him in a rocking chair, eyes half closed and head bent into a prayer book, she was swaying gently, murmuring a rueful prayer.

A bunch of colony pranksters passed B Block, hooting on paper horns and the sounds of their merriment invaded the flat from the night outside. As if in deference to the revellers who crowded the street, tonight had remained warm despite December. How thin Sheramai looked. No one who'd known her in her earlier days would have believed that this was Sheroo. Her sparse hair, tied in a knot and covered with a mathabana, showed only one strand that hung loose outside: grey. Her veins stood out on her hands that clutched the prayer book, as though it were some truly precious relic; long, bony hands, wiry from years of doing housework.

Fardoon scratched his shoulder through a tear in his sudra and stifled a yawn. How much longer would they have to wait up for Katie? Sheramai had almost finished praying. She whispered her concluding yashem vohus, got up from the rocking chair and went into the other half of the room which was partitioned off from this half that served as their sitting room. The passage that led to the kitchen at the rear was where Katie slept. From behind the wooden partition came the sound of the carved ancestral cupboard opening and being shut again. Fardoon couldn't look into that other half from where he was sitting. Nevertheless, he knew exactly what was happening behind the partition. The same routine that had been enacted every night for the last twenty-three years.

Every evening, after her prayers were done, Sheramai would first light the small lamp of coconut oil which was placed on a low table by her bed. Shutting her eyes, she would touch reverentially the two photo frames of Zarathustra, one of which was on the same table by the lamp, the other on the wall above her bed. Then into the old cupboard, carved with tigers' heads at its four top corners, would go Sheramai's prayer book, whose torn binding was repaired with scotch tape. With a creak the cupboard would be shut, and with a rumble the rusty Godrej Storwel would open next. Into this Sheramai would deposit her neatly folded mathabana, kiss a blurred and indistinct photograph saved from years ago, place it face down under a pile of old sudras (Sheramai was saving them for her own funeral rites), shut the cupboard and turn the key on it.

For twenty-three years now, every night, this had happened, and tomorrow would start the twenty-fourth. Fardoon's head was slightly furrowed as he counted the years. He had nothing against religion, no, nothing at all. Often enough, he went to the agiari at the corner of their lane and prayed for an hour, if he felt like it. But ever since that day of Rati's disappearance, Sheramai had spent all her spare time with her prayer book, either at home or in the agiari. That was not good, Fardoon felt. After all, you had to live for the living till your own day came. Everyone was not dead yet. He had said this many times to her. After all, hadn't it been a great shock for him as well? But he had coped. Yet every time he brought up the matter with Sheramai, she grew harsh and sullen and cursed him bitterly; as though he were the prime cause of her grief.

Tonight, there was an extra creak from the other side of the room; it wasn't a part of the nightly routine and for a moment puzzled Fardoonji. Then he recognized it. The medicine chest.

'What's wrong, Sheramai?' he called out.

After a long while she murmured, 'Nothing.'

Fardoon frowned; hesitated, then asked again,

'But what tablets are you taking?'

The room remained as silent as a tomb.

Outside, though, more horns bleated, drunken laughter seeped in through the thin walls of the flat, more jarring than ever, as though revellers had lost patience with the new year for tarrying thus.

Someone impatiently depressed a car horn for half a minute. Other vehicles contributed to the cacophony with more honking. Was there a traffic jam building up at Grant Road junction?

'Wind the clock in the kitchen for me, Fardoonji. It's stopped since morning. Tomorrow I'll be off to the agiari early.'

Sheramai was a tall woman. She could easily have wound it herself, but this task did not number among her personal chores, which were very numerous in any case. Winding the pendulum clock was a man's work, though it was more delicate a task than it might seem. Ah yes, thought Fardoon to himself, preparing to rise from his chair. Tomorrow is Adibesroj. I should drop in at the agiari too, a little later in the morning.

He stood up carefully, scratching himself on his thigh through his crumpled, long-cloth pyjamas. He was a big man who carried himself in a funny, bumbling sort of way; he shuffled towards the kitchen in his rubber slippers. Pausing in the passage, he observed: that heap of old newspapers, that collection of empty Dalda tins—why have they been stored at all? Must sell them off to the raddiwalla before they start breeding cockroaches. He groped for the light switch in the kitchen, and flicked it on.

The clock had stopped at ten to three. The kitchen was large, and served as their dining room as well. At one end was the square dining table over which, some years ago, Fardoon had nailed a plastic tablecloth. Still durable as ever, the plastic had only slightly frayed at the corners. On the table stood an empty beer bottle with a little foam in it, an unwashed glass, an empty plate with a potato wafer or two, and numerous fragments of uneaten crisps.

Fardoonji stretched his hand upwards and inserted the large ornamental key into the left aperture of the dial; when this spring felt almost fully wound, he moved the key to the other one, on the right side of the dial, and wound it once more. Next, manually and without hurrying, he gently pushed along the long hand clockwise to every half-hour juncture, waiting patiently for it to toll the appropriate number of chimes. He rather enjoyed the mellow resonance of the sounding tine, keeping count of the unhurried, silvery taps of the little hammer that lodged in the heart of the clock's mechanism. Lovely and precise.

Fardoonji had been bilious all evening and, while winding the clock, feeling its spring grow taut under his fingers, a small fart escaped him. He felt some relief. Now he set the hands: it was almost ten, five to, in fact. Then, a slight push to the pendulum, and the clock began ticking again with monotonous inflexibility as if claiming it had never stopped in the first place, nor a single moment passed unrecorded.

All that beer hadn't agreed with him. He should never have taken more than a glassful. But Sheramai had absolutely refused to touch it. She refused even a sip. He should have known. He shouldn't have gone out to get it at all. For so many years now, ever since Katie was born, they had started going out again, celebrating New Year's and other such days. For the baby's sake, Sheramai would say. But the baby had grown big now, and this year she had wanted to go out alone. She was at a party with college friends. Fardoonji had tried very hard to persuade Sheramai to go out this year. It's not good to think this way still, after so many years. You'll only bring us bad luck for the whole year. Come, I'll buy tickets for Netarwalla's new naatak . . . it'll be hilarious. But Sheramai was not to be moved. If I went out then, it was for baby's sake. Now the baby has gone out alone, I'll stay home.

Fardoon shook his head. Finally, he'd gone out and bought a bottle of beer and some wafers. At least if we are staying indoors we can have a little party here, just the two of us. But he'd had to drink up the beer and eat the wafers all by himself. Sheramai would not touch them.

Fardoonji sighed. True, the whole ghastly incident had been much more shattering for her, it would be. But then, ah, hadn't it been a great shock for him as well? For three months after it happened he had been severely ill, with a high fever that would not leave him. But once he recovered, he recovered. After all, one can't go on living in the past. There were others still alive. Fardoonji often said this to Sheramai. And every time he repeated it—he wasn't imagining it—he could feel her disgust, the hatred she felt for him.

About to switch off the light and leave the kitchen, his eyes turned in the direction of the cooking table with its Primus and Vellore wick stoves. The vessels containing Katie's dinner had not been covered. They'd had an early dinner, Sheramai and he, papeta nu gos and the extra dish, because it was New Year, of kheema cutlets.

Now the food was cold, and the gravy clotted with ghee.

Fardoonji looked around to find lids. Would Katie be back soon, before midnight, or just after? Perhaps he should leave the food over a slow flame so she could eat it hot as soon as she got back. She might be very hungry. But she wouldn't be back for a while yet. He only covered the two dishes and returned to his favourite easy chair with the extendable leg-rests . . . In the streets, the din was still raging.

'Sheramai, what time is Katie coming back?'

Rocking herself slowly in her chair, Sheramai's bony features were sharply etched by the dim light of the 40-watt bulb overhead. She spoke without looking up.

'Why do you ask me, Fardoonji?'

'I was only just wondering whether to put her food to heat or not.'

'Yes, yes, but why ask *me*?'

Sheramai stopped rocking and now gazed at her husband. He sensed a challenge in that look which made him uneasy.

'Who else should I ask then?'

'Anyone you like, Fardoonji, but not me. How should *I* know?' Sheramai looked away again. 'For months now, does she tell me anything, where she goes, what she does, anything?'

'But she told us, didn't she, she's at a friend's place enjoying a New Year's Eve party? All I'm asking is did she tell you what time she'd be back?'

'Why should I ask her what time she'll be back? Ha. I thought she'll definitely have told her papa . . . And who is this friend, where does he live? Papa knows everything, I'm sure . . .'

Sheramai's voice was bitterly sarcastic.

'Sheramai, I asked you a simple question, now all this . . . I wish I had not spoken,' Fardoon flopped resignedly into his easy chair and took up the morning's *Jame*. But Sheramai would not accept that as her cue to be silent.

'No, no. Oh no, no need to read the paper two-two times in a day. Why stop talking now? After all, how's the evening to get along if we just sit dumb? You wanted so to entertain me, didn't you?'

'Better to read the newspaper a hundred times than talk to you. That's all I have to say.' Fardoonji muttered angrily without lowering the screen of newsprint he had raised against his spouse's ire.

'That's all?' she mimicked him, intent on quarrelling. 'But why not say some more, Fardoonji?'

Now Fardoon lowered the newspaper, incensed.

'So you are bent on spending New Year's Eve mewling and ranting? If you want bad luck so much then bad luck won't disappoint you. Go ahead, that's all I can say to you.'

'That's all I can say, that's all I can say,' she imitated him again with savage derision. 'But why not say some more, Fardoonji? Have you no feelings for your family, even though you share the flat with us? When you feel like it you want a party. Otherwise, all day you'll bury your nose in your stamp album and even forget to eat. That's all right for you. It's I who have to meet the neighbours. *I* have to listen to what they have to say about your daughter, not you. *I* have to . . .'

At the mention of his stamp album, Sheramai's raving and ranting faded into the distance and, almost unawares, Fardoon's own thoughts found refuge in a deserted and very private corner of his mind . . .

~

Long ago, when Fardoon was still a boy scout, Cawasmama, his only bachelor uncle had taken him home after a meeting of ex-troopers. There in his ramshackle flat at Paowalla Gali, Cawasmama had shown him his private collection of stamps, and given him books on philately to read. Philately and Shakespeare were the two great passions in Cawasmama's life and one of them he had bequeathed to his nephew, Fardoon. It was said in the family that Cawas could quote large portions of any play you asked him to. He knew all the sonnets by heart, too, for Shakespeare was all he read, and he believed it was enough for any man's lifetime.

Fardoon looked at the yellowed photograph of his uncle under the glass top of the teapoy. Yes, even in his own recollection of years ago, Cawasmama had been very tall and very fair. Fardoon's father, Nusly, always said Cawas was the true European of the family. Cawasmama's last days were spent in abject poverty, at the mercy of the beneficence of his relatives. Yet, always a true European. It was said that to his dying day, even if he just went down to the Irani restaurant for a cup of tea, he was never seen without his tie-suit.

Cawasmama had died when Fardoon was only fifteen, and it turned out in his will that he had left Fardoon his entire stamp collection, a sprawling lifetime's effort. From that day, Fardoon himself developed a great interest in stamp-collecting and in his own way had become quite an authority on philately. When the time came for Fardoon to retire from his job in the insurance agency, he decided not to ask for an extension—possibly, they might not have granted it even had he asked—and now he spent all his free time with his albums.

Fardoonji was startled out of his reverie by a sharp burst of crackers from the direction of C Block. Sheramai was aware that he hadn't been listening to her. A faint smile appeared on her lips as she saw him start, and she shook her head, saying softly, 'Dream, dream, Fardoonji, what else do you know to do?'

Fardonji shifted uneasily in his easy chair, ignoring her remark. She seemed calmer now. It was five past eleven, he saw from the clock on the wall. He wondered how it was he could not remember hearing it strike eleven counts. After a while he said, 'Sheramai, you go to bed. I'll wait up for Katie.' But now Sheramai did not seem to hear, for now *she* was lost in her thoughts; the old couple sat in silence, waiting for their daughter to return home.

Unexpectedly, the light in the room flickered a few times. Fardoonji looked up at the bulb and frowned. He looked at it steadily for a few minutes, but it didn't flicker again.

It was not a cold night, but still, Fardoonji felt the need to get up and fetch his striped night-shirt from the wooden clothes horse which stood behind the partition. Before putting it on, he sniffed at it, and decided that tomorrow it must go in the washing. Then, he asked Sheramai, 'Shall I get you your shawl, Sheramai? Cover yourself with it, you may catch a chill.'

But Sheramai merely shook her head. Fardoonji sat down again; more time passed.

'Sheramai, you have to get up early in the morning, didn't you say? Why don't you go in—'

She interrupted: 'Have you put out the light in the kitchen?'

'Of course I have,' he replied, slightly irritated that his kindly suggestion was interrupted before he could complete it.

'What's so "of course" about that? Do you know what our light bill was last month?'

'I paid it, didn't I?'

'You paid it, yes, but did you notice how much? Thirteen rupees! Do you have any idea how little is left in your bank account?'

'Not tonight, Sheramai, not tonight of all nights! It's New Years' Eve. Are we going to spend the final hours of the year squabbling in this manner?'

'What's so special about New Year's Eve, tell me? Tomorrow won't be different from today. How will the next year be different from this one?'

'It will,' said Fardoonji firmly.

'No, it'll be the same, Fardoonji. It'll be worse. Next year or the year after. We'll still be counting loose change, saving the crumbs. God knows how we are going to manage.'

'It's only a question of a year or two. Once Katie starts earning, things will be very different, don't forget.'

'Katie? Ha, don't pin your hopes on that girl. She'll be married and off, before you even know who the boy is.'

'Sheramai, don't! What nonsense are you talking?'

'What am I talking? How would you know, Fardoonji? You hide all day in the house, licking your stamps—'

'Hinges,' Fardoonji corrected her softly.

'Do you know what Bachoobai from opposite was saying to me about your Katie?'

'I don't want to hear what Bachoobai from opposite was saying, that vicious old backbiter and gossip. Let her throw herself in the well, burnt up with jealousy for everyone that she is.'

'Oh, so poor Bachoo is to throw herself in the well? And what about old Tehmina, whose nephew Rusi is? What about Silloo from C Block? All into the well? All liars and envious hags? Fardoonji, you are always defending that girl, and she is always defending you. A nice arrangement this is, don't think I haven't noticed. Why, just three days ago I saw her with my own eyes—'

'Sheramai—'

'Nowhere near her college. With a boy—at Gowalia Tank maidan.' Sheramai's sentence was cut short by a violent flickering of the light and suddenly, the room was plunged into darkness. Fardoonji stiffened in his seat and, without knowing it, his grip on the two armrests of his chair tightened. Suddenly, all the warmth of the night seemed to have dissipated and he shivered in the icy draught blowing in from the half-open window. His voice was tremulous and frightened, like that of a child who wakes up in the night and finds he is alone.

'Sheramai—'

'It's all right, Fardoonji,' Sheramai's voice was low and soothing. She got up from her rocking chair and very casually went up to the window. She peered out and said, 'All the buildings', the compound lights have gone, too. It's a major power failure.'

Then she groped her way around the partition into the other half of the room where, a while ago, by the photo frame of Zarathustra, she had lit a small coconut oil lamp. She picked it up delicately, and taking small careful steps, brought it into the sitting room and placed it on the window sill. As she made her way back to her rocking chair, she put her hand on Fardoonji's shoulder and said softly, 'It's all right, Fardoonji. The lights will soon be back.'

Fardoonji started breathing more easily once the lamp had been moved to their room. The tiny wick flickered and threw long shadows into every corner. Every time a slight breeze lifted the patched curtain at the window, the shadows in the room would quiver convulsively, as if gripped by a terrible agony. Fardoonji pulled out the wooden leg-rest of his chair to its full length, and raised his left leg onto it. It emitted a painful squeak. Outside in the streets, the crowds seemed possessed by the night; its pitch-blackness gave refuge to their frenzy. The clocks in the city approached midnight, the paper horns shrilled and tooted and yelped with added fury, and from the distance came a constant gabble of carousing voices and drunken laughter.

But in the shabby little room where they sat, there was a hush. For a while, the flame glowed steadily. Then Sheramai spoke, her voice low and hoarse.

'So Fardoonji—'

Fardoonji's head was bent. He looked up.

'H'm?'

'What shall we talk about then, Fardoonji?'

Fardoon didn't answer. He looked away. After a while, he said, 'We can talk about . . . old times, can't we, Sheramai? Long ago . . . so many years have passed us by . . . Do you remember them?'

'Remember? What's there to remember in old times?' Perhaps there was a hint of irony in her tone, but Fardoon didn't let her dwell on it.

'Years ago, Sheramai, when Katie was still growing up . . . even before. Do you remember the Sunday matinees we sometimes saw with Katie? The best tickets upstairs were only ten annas, Sheramai . . .'

He looked up. Her face was expressionless, staring at the floor. He went on,

'And after that, if you didn't feel like cooking, some Sundays we would stop at A-1 and have their curry-rice, remember?'

'Ah yes, that's right . . .'

'You do remember, don't you, Sheramai?'

'Sometimes we saw a serious film which Katie was bored with: then her tricks would start. She would clutch at her stomach and groan, saying she had to go for number two, but Fardoonji, as soon as I took her to the toilet, she would fall into convulsions of giggling and say, "Fooled you".'

Fardoonji laughed, 'What a little imp she used to be. A real devil.'

'How you pampered her, Fardoonji. You would come home

from work with your pockets full of sweets and she would eat and eat till her teeth ached.'

'Her favourites were those éclairs from Parisian, remember?'

'The little angel really made the days fly past. For a while, I think I was completely happy again.'

'You were, Sheramai, you were. You even agreed to come to Matheran, remember, so Katie could see the place?'

A weary smile appeared on Sheramai's face.

'How excited she was that first morning when she spotted a monkey in the sanatorium garden. He came back every morning at sunrise and watched her from a distance. She decided to call him Piloo, after your cousin, whom she said he resembled.'

'Poor Piloo. It's true, he had the same nervous air. Tried so hard for a woman to marry, but never, never found one . . .'

'It was difficult for you to get leave often, Fardoonji, but whenever you could we'd take her somewhere. That was in the days when she was young and things were cheaper.'

'. . . the poor chap died three years ago, a seedy, bug-bitten bachelor, in that hotel at Grant Road, what was it called? Ah yes, London Hotel.'

'How many years since we last visited Udwada?'

'Matheran. She always enjoyed Matheran the best, always.'

'Her tastes were like my own. Definitely, they were . . . Did we spoil her Fardoonji? Did we spoil her with too much loving?'

'Do you remember that time she went off alone for a walk and did not return for hours? What a fright we got. You were weeping and I didn't know what on earth to do.'

'Then she came back . . . ah, we wouldn't stop kissing her, we wouldn't let her go.'

'You remember everything clearly, Sheramai.'

'Yes, Fardoonji. I remember everything well. As if it were yesterday.'

The easy chair creaked, as Fardoonji shifted in it wearily. How many years was it since she last called him Fardoon? How many years since he stopped calling her Sheroo?

~

The noise from the jubilant streets laid siege to the thin-walled, two-room flat of old Fardoonji and Sheramai. It was almost midnight. In the room, the flame of the coconut oil lamp danced spasmodically, like a paraplegic who had decided to take part in the night's festivities. The thoughts of the old couple dredged through the debris of the past, spent moments, now only faintly recalled.

Fardoonji's stomach made a gurgling sound.

'But Sheramai, do you not remember the times before these, when Katie was just born?'

Sheramai was sitting upright in her rocking chair, her hands in her lap. She was staring directly in front of her, as though she had not heard Fardoonji speak.

'. . . even earlier, I mean, before Katie was born . . .'

'Fardoonji—' in Sheramai's voice was a plea, a warning, but Fardoonji didn't heed it.

'I remember them, Sheramai, I remember them well. Don't you remember that fortnight in summer we spent at Panchgani?'

Sheramai kept her silence, and Fardoonji asked again,

'Don't you, Sheramai?'

'Fardoonji, when have we ever been to Panchgani?' Sheramai spoke stonily, as she continued to stare into shadows.

Fardoonji feigned shock.

'What, such a poor memory? You are really growing old, if you can forget Panchgani so easily, Sheramai! Don't you remember, we'd—'

'Never, we have never been to Panchgani, Fardoonji.'

'I am amazed at you. We stayed at the Albless Sanatorium, a mile up in the hills . . .'

'Leave it, Fardoonji, now leave it.' Sheramai's voice betrayed agitation. She was breathing hard. 'I don't *remember*!'

'Oh come, Sheroo, of course you remember. The memory of Panchgani should be a happy one for us. Why try to forget that? Don't you remember we'd gone there with—'

'Stop, Fardoonji, I've forbidden you to mention the name!'

But the more anguish Fardoon's inquest of the past caused his wife, the more relentless and obsessive it became, as though he were deriving some vain satisfaction in tormenting her.

'Forbidden? You are a child, Sheramai. Even this year, then, there is no change.'

'Stop it, Fardoonji, I warn you!' Sheramai hissed from between clenched teeth.

'Merely her name can get you hysterical? For twenty-three years you have put her little soul in fetters and exiled its memory, all mention of her name from the house of her birth. Tomorrow begins the twenty-fourth. How many more years will this insanity continue?'

Fardoon's voice droned on in the night with a slight nasal twang, as if he knew his lines by rote, a part of some devious ritual he was now beginning to enjoy.

'If you have any sense, Fardoonji, stop.' Sheramai's voice was distraught, her eyes red.

'One night twenty-three years ago has gnarled and infected the rest of your life. Every shred of these past years you have soaked in deathly gloom. You have made things miserable for us, Sheramai.'

'For your own sake, Fardoonji, I warn you. Stop!'

'Shall we not talk about that night, Sheramai, twenty-three years ago? Every new year reminds us of it, for it was a night like this one . . .'

At this, Sheramai froze. She had turned deathly pale and her voice had fallen to a whisper.

'Be careful what you say, Fardoonji. You will only bring it on yourself, you—fool!' But Fardoonji wasn't listening.

'We decided that night to try a new Chinese restaurant that had just opened at Fort. After that, there was that film, that ill-fated Abbot and Costello film we so much wanted to show to—'

'If you utter her name, Fardoonji . . .'

Sheramai's voice was husky and barely audible; but her nails dug deep into the threadbare cushion she was sitting on.

'Upset about a name, Sheramai? Such a nice name . . .'

'Fardoonji—'

'Do you remember, it was I who suggested it when she was born?'

'Leave it!'

And can I not even say it now? I love that name . . .'

'Fardoonji!'

'Rati. What a lovely name. Rati, Rati, Rati . . .'

'Don't you dare take her name, you—' Sheramai's voice shrieked into the night, 'you butcher! How I hate you!'

'What! What did you say?' Fardoonji gasped, unbelieving.

'Butcher, I said butcher! You, it was you, child-killer, know it since you must, you lost my child, not I,' Sheramai screamed, burning with a rage of years. Fardoonji was stunned, he opened his mouth, but no words came. Then he hid his face in his hands.

Just then the clocks in the city struck twelve and its streets were filled with the sound of squeaky paper-horns the balloon-man had sold. From afar came the funereal sound of fog-horns from the ships at sea, groaning like an ancient underwater beast grown tired and rheumatic from dampness. And in the room, as the curtains lifted in the breeze, the lamp on the window sill cringed and glowered.

Sheramai uttered a sob and shook her head in denial.

'No, no, Fardoonji, not true. I didn't mean that, I . . .'

'I heard you, Sheramai, I heard you clearly . . .'

'No, I meant . . .'

What was she on about? Lies. Of course, all lies. I remember everything exactly as it happened.

New Year's Eve. Twenty-three years ago. Gateway of India. Midnight. Teeming crowds, pushing, jostling, elbowing to get a better view of the fireworks on the ships at sea . . . Sheramai—yes, it *was* Sheramai—was holding Rati's hand, craning to get a good view herself. It took her God knows how long, a minute—to realize that Rati had slipped out of her grip—perhaps to gain vantage ground to watch the spectacle from.

Where was she now, where was Rati? Rati rati rati rati, where are you, then the hysteria mounted, searching, screaming, dashing about, where was she, Rati, oh the horror of it, where was the girl, where are you Rati . . .

But their voices had been drowned in the tumult of merriment, drunkenness, and good wishes for the new year. Till three in the morning the frantic search continued, then police, friends, newspapers, dragnets. . .

The body was never recovered; she was classified by the police as missing. But missing—where, what, how? Leaned over the parapet, drowned, trampled to death? No, no, that was not possible . . . Then kidnapped and crippled; taught to beg or . . . Oh God, no not that . . .!

The uncertainty, the ambiguity was more unbearable than death itself.

But *that's* how it happened. He had had nothing to do with it. Or he would have remembered . . . Could it be that— Oh no, no; in the end—just now—she admitted it was a lie. She had taken her words back. It wasn't true. No. Never could be . . .

~

Fardoonji rubbed his eyes. He felt a peculiar dryness in his mouth. The light in the room had come on. Sheramai was not in her rocking chair and the lamp on the window sill had burnt itself out.

Fardoonji became aware of a bristly, warm presence around him. He must have fallen asleep, and Sheramai had covered him with a blanket. Then Katie was not back yet? Fardoonji yawned and looked at the clock on the wall. Where *was* this girl now?

The night had grown colder and the streets were much quieter, but there were still occasional noises; the half-hearted shuffle of those returning home. The night had worked itself up to its peak and spilt over. Now what was left was only thirst, queasiness, unanswered questions waiting, like unwashed linen in the tub, to be doused in the light of morning.

Fardoonji could not remember clearly what had happened in the earlier part of the night. He remembered Sheramai had been quite upset, very upset about something. But she would be okay in the morning. This kind of thing happened sometimes, every now and then. A good night's sleep would do her good.

Fardoonji was deciding on going to bed himself, when there was a soft knocking on the door. He went up to it, shifted the tin bottle-lid which had been nailed over the peephole and peered out. He heaved a sigh of relief; then slid the bolt carefully so as not to wake Sheramai, and let Katie in. He said to her in a loud whisper, 'So late, baby? Go, your dinner is on the stove. Heat it, before eating.'

'I've eaten already. Thanks. Good night.' Katie nearly stumbled over Sheramai's rocking chair and disappeared into the back of the house. As she passed him, Fardoonji caught a whiff of stale whisky.

Well. Fardoonji was about to turn in, but from the next room came Sheramai's voice mumbling something. Ah, she was talking in her sleep again. He went up to her bed and whispered soothingly.

'It's all right, Sheramai, Katie's back safely. Now go to sleep.' He picked up her blanket which had slipped off her body and covered her with it.

Then, going back into the sitting room, he bolted the front door in three places. He shifted the rocking chair an inch to the left. He looked at the floor for a moment.

Then he switched off the light, and carefully groped his way into bed, thinking about a new set of stamps and a first day cover that the government would be releasing on Republic Day; it was called Orchids of India. He had seen a facsimile of the artwork in the *Jam-e-Jamshed* the previous morning.

Passion Flower
(A Fantasy)

In the human spirit, as in the universe, nothing is higher or lower; everything has equal rights to a common centre which manifests its hidden existence precisely through this harmonic relationship between every part and itself.

—Goethe, in an essay (1824)

For the life of him, Anand could never have explained why the old codger aroused such repugnance in him; not one to analyze his feelings, he hadn't given the question any thought.

Yet it was astounding how much irritation and anger had been building up in him towards the poor beggar ever since he moved into his new quarters. And that, without the latter's doing anything to annoy him, except for begging in his path. Well, Anand was in no mood to be apologetic about how he felt: at times, positively murderous.

When he set out to school, at 7.45 a.m. on most days, the old humbug was never around. Too canny to be caught out in bad weather, he studiously avoided the cold, gusty mornings. But later, when the sun was up, and Anand came home briefly during lunch break—his housekeeping Amma would have prepared and left behind some dosai, or a pot of soup for him—that horrible cloying whine would assault his senses; Anand would flinch in anticipation, hearing it almost before he actually did. Wrapped, as always, in a faded lungi and threadbare shawl, palm outstretched and flailing about, bowing low and repeatedly with exaggerated deference, the scoundrel would harass him without mercy.

Though Anand didn't understand a word of Tamil, the meaning of the beggar's loud and mournful bleating was impossible to miss. On several occasions, he *had* turned out his pockets for all the coins he could find. But once money exchanged hands, there was never any acknowledgement, not even the sham gratitude one expects of a supplicant. After glancing at the coins in his palm, the old fox would look away disdainfully, as though implying—too little, and long overdue anyway. And were he, Anand, to pass that way again in no more than a few minutes, a fresh dose of the same dirge-like moaning would be unleashed in his direction as though the contribution of a few minutes ago had never been made or received. Was he crazy? Dulled by habitual, mindless grubbing, or simply amnesiac?

One thing was certain: Anand wasn't exactly bleeding with compassion for the man. In fact, he rather wished this loud-mouthed potentate of the wayside could be deposed; swiftly, violently, if necessary, somehow prevented from further despoiling his brief hill sojourn.

He had taken on this teaching post for one semester only—true, the contract was extendable should he wish to stay on—but before he made up his mind on that, there were other things he had to figure out: essentially, which way his life was headed.

All this was new to him: the place, the school, the people, the language, even the local vegetation was unfamiliar. His home was Delhi. He had always lived in that city; studied there, married a girl he'd met during his college years; now his wife was expecting their first child.

Not everything had gone as smoothly it should have. A mysterious, unidentified fever had racked Pamela's body during her fifth week of pregnancy. At the time they hadn't even known she was expecting a baby; nor had their family physician, who had subdued the fever with fierce onslaughts of antibiotics. Chances of the foetus being affected—if not by the fever, then the drugs—should not be discounted, her gynaecologist had warned. He had prescribed investigations.

They were both young; there would be many more chances to have kids. At least, so he had argued. This pregnancy was mistimed, anyway. In fact, Anand had only just applied to a university in Colorado, USA, where he hoped to pursue a doctorate while teaching part-time. The university hadn't got back to him yet, but he was confident the post would be made available to him. They might even have agreed to accommodate his spouse, if she'd shown any interest in coming along,

When the time for having a child was right and propitious, they could plan his future sensibly; on a clean state, as it were. That was Anand's position. But Pamela was a devout Christian who had spent her childhood in a village in Old Goa, only a few kilometres from the Basilica of Bom Jesus; she would not dream of having an abortion.

The only other alternative was a battery of tests, fortnightly ultrasound scans and, of course, lots of prayer, all of which Pamela was already preoccupied with. Until he left Delhi, nothing untoward *had* been detected. But what should have been a happy few months for the young couple was marred by dispute and anxiety.

Anand prided himself greatly on his rationality, he found irrational behaviour, wherever he encountered it, infuriating; and here, his own wife was being totally unreasonable. What would they do if the child was born blind or even marginally defective? Every detail of a growing foetus can't be precisely monitored. Until a few weeks ago they could still have ended this high-tension drama. Now, even if they should discover some physical or mental deformity, how would it help? It was too late.

She had fought bitterly to hold her own.

'Oh, so you think you'll be doing the writing, is it,' she countered his arguments with savage irony, 'on a "clean slate"? You're even more egotistical than I thought, Anand. A child is a gift from God . . . *You* can't decide when to accept it, when not to; at *your* convenience, you fool!'

'*My* convenience?' shouted Anand, his raised voice reflecting his outrage, 'Oh *please*. In all this you're simply forgetting the child who'll be here with us soon . . . Will it be to his convenience—or hers—to be born blind? Or deaf? Or handicapped? Merely because his mother was too headstrong?'

'You simply lack any faith,' said Pamela. 'Let's just leave it.'

'Oh yes, I quite forgot about your private hotline,' said Anand.

'What?' asked Pamela, not sure if she'd heard him right.

'To God, I mean,' continued Anand with a grin, 'your sugar daddy who's guaranteed you a perfect offspring—non-shrink, non-crumple—insured, so to speak, by the offerings you send up every morning, isn't that right? That's the deal?'

'Oh shut up!' snapped Pamela. 'How crass can you be, unbeliever! Devil incarnate!'

Happily, that was one argument had ended in mirth rather than raw nerves. At least, she had a sense of the ridiculous, he was pleased to admit, and knew how to laugh at herself. But finally, that hadn't helped resolve their differences. Pamela decided to move—to her mother's place in Goa. She encouraged Anand to forget about her and the baby for a while, get on with his own work.

When he read in the papers of an opening at the L'Ecole Internationale for a lecturer in Botany, he immediately sent off his application. Not too many qualified teachers would be willing to leave the city for a remote hill station in South India. He needed time to himself. He had little patience with uncertainty; nor any for indecisiveness, incompetence or failure; the failure in this case, should something go wrong, would not be the infant's, but Pamela's own.

Once again a question Anand had never confronted with any degree of honesty stirred biliously in his gut, like a worm; momentarily, then slithered into that nervous unease he felt whenever a situation wasn't entirely in his control. Should the child be born with a handicap, needing serious rehabilitation, or lifelong help, would he be able to embrace it? Make all the sacrifices he would be called on to make? At the moment he could only feel disgust at the prospect of such self-imposed encumbrance. Life was no joke, he had always believed; when lived intelligently, artfully, and with a little cunning, it brought success and success, happiness. There was little room in his scheme of things for matters of faith. Nothing came on a platter, even if you prayed hard for it. He knew this from experience; much work and considerable manipulation of his own circumstances—and others'—had preceded his getting even as far as he had.

Some years ago, he had believed that Pamela shared his beliefs about rational behaviour; that's what had brought them together. But clearly, he had been wrong. Passion had taken a step backwards in their lives the moment Pamela announced her baby, and that she was determined to keep it. If on top of everything else that hadn't quite worked out right in the marriage, he was saddled with a disabled kid . . . he'd never be able to accept it. He had tried to make her see reason, but with no success. In any case, the time for arguments was over.

(ii)

The tourist season had been terribly noisy. The narrow lanes of the old hill station could accommodate only so many vehicles. There were vicious traffic snarls which the couple of policemen on duty weren't able to sort out without recourse to excessive hysteria; besides, tourists brought along their nasty city habits of speeding whenever the road was clear and honking incessantly, even if nothing was blocking their way.

Dozens of honeymooning couples, large extended families, whole busloads of college or school kids came up the hill during these three months using every means of private and public transport to catch a glimpse of the famed evergreen forests, shiver deliciously in the tantalizing mist, delight in the bands of wild monkeys who turned tricks for morsels of stale sandwiches or rancid potato chips before driving back to the safety and warmth of the plains, after littering the pristine hills with their garbage.

Again, why had this man chosen to position himself just a few feet away from Anand's garden gate? The answer to that question was evident if he would just stop being paranoid—a fork in the road just a few feet away led to a popular lookout called Suicide Point which was a favourite with tourists with literally hundreds of them trooping that way every day, beguiled by its name and reputation; none of them was allowed to pass without the clamorous dotard giving pursuit. During the three months of the tourist boom, Anand thought the scrounger must make a pretty packet.

No different from other vagrants who begged at entry-points to promenades and valley-views in this popular hill resort, this one was only rather advanced in age. The place was crawling with beggars, though none so persistent or bullying in the scramble for alms. It wasn't his business, of course, how much the man earned—if such harassment of the public could be called earning! But, apart from that, there was something so revolting about the man's antics, his manipulative efforts to elicit sympathy or embarrassment in passers-by that Anand, who was exposed almost daily to this tasteless shamming, felt an instinctive hatred for the man. This was undoubtedly enhanced by his own helplessness—he knew that there was nothing he could do to get him to move some place else. Rarely had life left Anand feeling so impotent and frustrated.

His only release was to imagine ways in which he could rid himself of this pest. A sharp nudge delivered en passant, Anand took pleasure in fantasizing, or an exceptionally sustained and icy draft, were all it might take to tip the dodderer into the valley of the next world! In quasi-conscious monologues, Anand had worked out precise stratagems for luring him down the path to Suicide Point and up to its protective paling; then, the mighty heave!

It wasn't as though Anand hadn't tried to reason with him. They didn't share a language but, on at least one occasion, he had employed a kind of mock-pidgin to communicate with the beggar, reinforced by expansive gesturing:

'Look, I live here, you know,' he had pointed to his cottage. 'Teaching in school. Local, local—not tourist. Going school, coming back, five times daily. How I give money every time? Tourists having lot of money, please catching tourist . . .'

While Anand was addressing him, the old fellow squinted nervously through the soda-bottle lenses perched on his mole-infested nose; an attentive and embarrassed look in his eyes suggested that he had got the gist of what was being said. But no sooner had Anand spoken his bit and walked on, than the pathetic whine of craving rang out behind him.

What angered Anand more than anything else was the beggar's pretended disability—he was old all right, but there were others around who were genuine cripples, with amputated or diseased limbs. This fellow didn't seem to have much wrong with him, yet he kept drawing attention to his one spindly shin, patting and squeezing it at intervals, as though to tell the world that this, alas, was the chief source of all his woes; but even the absurdly exaggerated limping he resorted to while giving chase to potential alms givers reverted to normal walking, Anand observed, once the intended quarry had out-walked him.

Now that kind of play-acting was just crooked and disgusting, thought Anand. On one occasion, he had been trying to ignore and resolutely out-walk the nuisance, when he spied his school's vice principal at a window in his quarters, closely observing this apparent heartlessness. For Anand, it had been a moment of great confusion and chagrin; the VP, too, had an awkwardly stiff walk, and needed a stick to support himself.

That afternoon Anand, not able to resist an extra helping of Amma's deliciously sweet pongal, stretched out for a bit after lunch on the settee in his living room. When he opened his eyes again, the interior of the small stone cottage had darkened. A light drizzle was pattering outside, a gently belligerent breeze roughing up the young frangipani outside his window. He hadn't meant to sleep at all, but his wristwatch showed that he had for at least fifteen minutes. Roused suddenly from too brief a nap, Anand felt as though sleep hadn't quite relinquished its grip on him; as if a part of him that had wandered out while he dozed hadn't slipped back nimbly enough when he opened his eyes, into that recess of heart or brain where it normally lodged.

His class of Botany twelfth-graders would be waiting. They might even have trooped down to the requisitioned school bus, impatient to start their fieldtrip. Or wondering perhaps, if for some unknown reason, it had been cancelled?

Scrunching past the young acacias in his leaf-strewn garden, Anand breathed in the soft fragrance of rain-washed leaves. Just then, he remembered the tattered threads of a dream that had capriciously strayed into his after-lunch nap. In the dream, too, he had been a teacher; but at a special school for disabled children. The class he was expected to take charge of comprised a grotesque assembly of physically and mentally challenged kids. There were far too many of them, a confused milling mass of contorted, lopsided beings—even more in number than there were chairs in the room for them to sit on. Many of them looked as though they might need help just to be able to sit! He was appalled: he hadn't been trained for this kind of work, how could he possibly cope?

With fatal inexorability, even at that hour of afternoon, the beggar was standing firmly entrenched in his usual spot, bent almost double with self-deprecation, bowing over and over again; the road was deserted: evidently he had been waiting for Anand to emerge. On hearing the clink of the garden gate being shut his wailing grew considerably in volume. Now Anand wasn't quite feeling himself; besides, he was late for class. Ignoring the beggar, he walked briskly past; but the old man, obstreperous as ever, limped after him, frantically swaying both body and arms while producing that guttural full-throated plea in Tamil, presumably for compassion and generosity—though it sounded to Anand as though someone were sawing away at his scrawny neck with a blunt knife.

Turning on him with a coldly deliberate ferocity, Anand swore: 'What's wrong with you, buddhe? Do I look like a bloody tourist to you? Why do you keep bothering me like this, day after day . . .?' Then he muttered to himself, but audibly, 'Fucking arsehole . . .'

The brutality of his tone was not misread. Had there been a conveniently sized stone lying in his path, Anand might have seized it, brought it crashing down on that wispy pate, he was that indignant. But his words produced no less devastating an effect. Something strange happened to the poor beggar: he froze. In silence he seemed visibly to wilt, like a plant that's been deprived of air in a shuttered room. Anand glared at him for one moment longer, before hurrying on; but in that moment he noticed something that made him regret the vehemence of his outburst—a faint trembling of aged, cracked lips. He had given the old chiseller a real fright. Immediately afterwards, the momentary regret passed and Anand was pleased to note that the awful trademark caterwauling he had been unconsciously waiting for hadn't resumed even after he had reached the school gate.

That wrathful instant had had a cathartic effect on Anand, too. Finally, he found himself clear-headed and wide awake; his wristwatch showed he was no more than twelve minutes late; the school's mini-bus was waiting in the parking lot. The driver and his students had already taken their seats. When he boarded the bus himself, with an apology for being late, Anand felt a sense of satisfaction: this was the only way perhaps, he thought to himself, the old wretch could be made to lay off.

(iii)

The school's mini-van began to move. The students seemed relieved, as though they had secretly worried that some arbitrary but official caprice might call off the outing at the very last minute; only after the bus had cleared the school gates, and begun its bumpy ascent towards Perumalmalai, did everyone relax; the atmosphere became infected with the charm and jollity of a class picnic. A small class, only nine boys and two girls, were in the bus with Anand, all of whom had opted for Biology as a major for their final year at school—which included a compulsory paper in Botany.

'Certainly, certainly,' Banerji had agreed immediately when he had met him in his office two days ago, expressly to seek permission for the field trip. 'I can see the diversionary value of such a trip. But *now*, with the finals only two months away?

Banerji's brand of cagey courtesy meant you never quite knew where you stood with him. Only when he absolutely needed to, Anand spent a few minutes with the VP, resorting to amicable banter which meshed unobtrusively with the latter's verbosity. A linguist, who was fluent in eight languages including Tamil, Banerji was reputed to be a snitch according to staff-room gossip, an informer for the Board who spied on the private behaviour of teachers. At his most recent interview with him, Anand had been moved to protest,

'Not merely diversionary, I should hope,' he had retorted acidly, 'they'll be learning something, too, from this outing.'

'Well, you know how it is, Mahendroo. I have no choice but to follow the set procedure for such requests . . . I'm just a functionary here, after all, please understand.'

'All it means is one afternoon's excursion,' Anand had said, for once not attempting to conceal his indignation. This was meant to be a 'progressive' school, where teachers were encouraged to innovate, 'find more exciting ways of teaching'. 'Is it essential to be so bureaucratic about anything at all?—And if you would just look at their timetable, you'll see they won't have to miss any classes. My students have a number of "frees" that afternoon.'

'Once board exams come around, poor children, there's so much pressure on them . . .' Banerji's sentence had trailed off dreamily, as if he weren't speaking to Anand at all. 'You understand this better than I do, I'm sure . . . but, Mahendroo, my hands are tied,' he had continued more animatedly. 'I am asked to account for every single hour which is spent outside of school routine, every single paisa of additional expense. I regret the day I accepted this post. The Board just won't let me be. Every Tom, Dick and Hari feels it's his right to interfere . . . I just wasn't meant for a desk job, I suppose. I should have remained a sportsman . . . I've told you my story, haven't I?'

'Oh yes,' Anand had said hastily, 'about your tennis career. Very unfortunate, sir . . .' he had not been able to resist adding, 'though that was a long time ago . . .'

In his youth, Banerji had been a tennis pro who had, apparently, made it all the way to Wimbledon for a tournament. In London traffic, however, before he could play his scheduled match, he had been knocked down by a black cab—so the story went. Operations on his fractured hip, done at a large public hospital in Waterloo had been thoroughly botched, the imperfect results of which were still visible every time he walked.

'You know me, Mahendroo,' Banerji had continued, now

eager to mollify him, 'I'm all for any brush with reality. I fear sometimes that isolated here on top of this mountain our children are cut off too much from reality . . . And when you're teaching Botany, what could be better than to see and touch and smell those flowers you are talking about . . . We live in the midst of nature, alas, yet have so little contact with it. None of my business, by the way, but you do go there quite often—to this spot? So I've heard . . .'

'Only in my spare time. And on my own bike,' Anand had said coldly. 'This is the first time I'll be taking the children. By school-bus.'

'Of course, of course, you have every right to. I was only asking how your own research is progressing,' the V.P. had said, backing down hastily. 'I, for one, hope you will be with this school for a long, long time to come. Good teachers are so difficult to come by. And here, I'm sure, you'll find enough time for some serious research.'

It was annoying to discover that Banerji had instinctively latched on to an idea he had secretly nursed ever since he joined the school. In his spare time, Anand would often be in the school's reference library, mulling over a set of books on flora in the Palani Hills. (Had Banerji been spying on him?) There were many species in these volumes which were 'believed to be extinct', but Anand believed otherwise. Given the climate, altitude and rank exuberance of nature in these parts, there was a fairly good chance that a few of them might, in some pocket of the forest, be proliferating again.

Well one, at least? That one was all he needed to zero in on. It had rapidly grown into an obsessive preoccupation. To find, while he was here, one plant which the world's herbaria claimed was extinct, but on which he, Anand Mahendroo, would pen a research paper documenting its existence in a corner of South India where the species still flourished. That would be something to make the guys at Colorado sit up and take notice, maybe even offer him a research fellowship.

'It's not a very large class, is it, the one you are thinking of taking out? Do you need a chaperone to accompany you?

'They're all twelfth graders, quite capable of looking after themselves.'

'Well, that's settled then. I'll see to it there's no problem about the bus . . .'

Anand had discovered this location quite by a chance during a weekend hike he had been obliged to chaperone for a class of eighth-graders. He didn't know the name for it, but somewhere between Perumalmalai and Mellpalam a small valley dipped between the hills, through which a perennial stream flowed; despite the poor rainfall of these months, it was still in full flow. The variety of local flora he had found in that location fascinated him, and he had thought his students might have fun, too, trying to identify some specimens.

After twenty minutes of driving along the undulating ghat road, the bus took a by-pass on to a dirt track, throwing up a lot of dust; another five minutes or so, and they ground to a halt. Mist had risen sharply from the valley below; all the multi-coloured grasses, herbs, climbers, trees, and branches were shrouded in an ominous chiaroscuro of grey and white. The air had turned chill. Everything seemed once removed from immediate reality, glazed by an ethereal, ghost-like beauty . . .

pines, firs, eucalypti, gorse, silver birches, large-flowered magnolias, the spooky contours of the bent European elders and so many others which he didn't even know the names of. When the driver parked the bus by the side of the road and switched off the engine, the silence grew palpable. No one was chattering. The most giddy-headed of the students had grown sombre, impressed by the beauty of the place they had reached.

'All of you remembered your walking shoes, I hope?' whispered Anand, glancing at their feet. Then in a more normal tone of voice, 'We're lucky it hasn't rained for almost a month . . . or this gully would have been trickier to negotiate. Still, let's go very slow. If you need help, don't hesitate to ask; or please just help one another as we go along.'

'I must warn you,' in the silence, Banerji's bullying threat reverberated in his ears, as from a great distance. 'It's difficult terrain. Whoever organizes the field trip must take responsibility for any mishaps. Seven years ago there was an accident. Son of a minister in the ruling government, there was hell to pay. So much fuss, so much fussing I tell you over one sprained ankle . . .! Don't let the children out of your sight, Mahendroo!' he had yelled, just as Anand was leaving his plush office.

But all they did that afternoon, once they had walked down to a clearing near where the stream flowed, was sit huddled on the grass, playing a quiz game devised by Anand. The teacher divided his students into two teams; then, using botanical terms which the students had come across in their texts and should have been familiar with, he gave each of the teams, alternately, a chance to point out one instance of plant or tree or specimen from their immediate surroundings which illustrated the meaning of the word in question. If one team couldn't provide the correct answer, the same word moved on to the other team.

'Glabrous . . .' called Anand, beginning with a fairly common term, of which there were any number of examples around. The students went into a huddle to confirm the meaning of the word, before Shailaja picked her way to a small shrub with purple flowers, whose leaves were smooth and unencumbered.

'Very good,' said Anand. 'Glabrous is just another word for smooth-surfaced. And two more points for anyone who can tell me the name of that glabrous herb.' But no one was quite so knowledgeable. 'It belongs to a family of creepers called Drymaria, you'll see a lot of it growing wild in these parts, all through the year.'

'Tomentose . . .' was his next choice of word, but Team 'B' had no idea what it meant.

And the term passed back to Team 'A'. Christopher, the pimply American lad, knew what he was looking for when he stood up, and quickly found a hibiscus shrub, whose leaves were thick with a woolly, matted down.

Androphore . . . gynandrous, and so on, the game continued for a while. Everyone enjoyed learning botanical terminology in the outdoors. Even when the light began to drop, no one seemed to want to leave.

Finally, it was Anand who drew their attention to the time; for he knew, quite as well as the students themselves, that if they weren't back within the sombre, stone halls of their dormitories by 8 p.m., the mess would close and they'd have to go without any dinner. But Immanuel of Team 'B' was being obstinate.

'Not fair, sir!' he protested, 'Why should we have one chance less? Just give us one more word, sir, and we'll equal their score!'

Already the light had become too poor for anyone to be able to pick out the minute features of a leaf or plant; but obviously Immanuel wanted some more time in that darkening vale off Mellpalam.

Humouring the boy, Anand threw him an unfamiliar term—'cordate'—which flummoxed not just Immanuel, but everyone else in both teams. Then, getting to his feet, to indicate that the field trip was finally at an end, he pointed out the meaning of the word in the heart-shaped leaves of clumps of Viola growing in abundance around the very mound of earth on which Team 'B' had been seated.

'Cordate: heart-shaped,' explained Anand. 'Remember that the next time you send someone a Valentine's Day card.' Some of the boys and girls tittered.

In darkness, once they were all seated in the bus, Anand did a head-count. For a moment, he started in fright, for there seemed one member less in the group than they had started out with. But he counted again, walking down the aisle between the seats; to his relief, he found one of the boys curled up on the last seat with his eyes closed.

'Not well?' Anand nudged the boy's shoulder.

Rohit, the boy in question, opened his eyes a moment and grunted, 'I'm okay . . . just hungry.'

Then, dreamily, he closed his eyes again; whether the boy was pretending to sleep while continuing to gaze at him through lightly shut eyelids, or had in fact drifted off, Anand couldn't tell. The driver was warming the engine; when Anand nodded, he shifted into gear and they began to move.

(iv)

A quality of silence enveloped the little hill town unlike anything Anand had experienced before. Suddenly, everyone had left. The narrow streets, once bristling with cars, buses and tourists, now wore a deserted look.

Occasionally, a fruit-picker with a headload of bananas, avocados or pears climbed up the slope from the forest; or the old cowherd, who supplied milk to some of the school's cottages including Anand's own, was seen leading his heifer by a stout rope to her grazing grounds. For minutes on end after that no one passed by at all. The air had turned distinctly colder, and the sky was almost always grey and overcast.

The stillness and hush were actually audible now, mused Anand, not just the chirruping of birds or rustling of leaves, one could hear even the fleet-footed scuttling of squirrels in trees, or so he would have liked to believe . . . The aura of serenity absorbed and elated him, cushioning him with peace. He felt an unmistakable sense of satisfaction; then, he thought guiltily of his wife, Pamela. There had been no news from her in three weeks. She would be big with his baby, now entering her eighth month . . . had he got the dates right? He tried to imagine what she might look like in so advanced a state of pregnancy; but the image that flashed in his mind was gross: a caricature, evoking distaste rather than tenderness.

Being squeezed into the straitjacket of fatherhood in no more than a few weeks was an alarming prospect. He preferred not to think about it. His baby would become a part of this world at most in a month from now. It's true he *was* terribly excited, but with matters quite apart from imminent parental bliss.

Only yesterday, Anand had come across three varieties of the *Passiflora* family flowering in the same dense thicket, close to one another, not far from where he had taken his students on their field trip. These varieties weren't so uncommon, of course: the *linnaeus*, the *cerulea*, the *edulis* . . . he had gone back to the library to confirm their identities. But he could sense the trail getting warmer. If all its family relations were thriving, why not, then, the one cousin he was looking for? His search was for *Passiflora boliviana*, once rampant in Argentina and Peru at heights of 2,000 metres and above, but which had disappeared since. The creeper was last recorded as having been spotted in the Upper Palanis by J. R. Fraser, a British explorer and botanist, in 1934. For several decades now, all over the world, it was considered extinct.

From wordy botanical descriptions, and a rare photograph reproduced in a mildewed volume he had found in the school library, he knew exactly what it looked like: its vines, their axillary tendrils, the solitary white flowers with purple filaments, sweet and pulpy berries—he could almost taste those berries. Somehow, Anand had become obsessed with this one particular plant, believing intuitively it was still around. Why else, when speeding across deserted mountain paths on his motorbike, did his mind swerve at every blind curve, slowing almost to a halt, even though his bike moved on—in anticipation of an epiphany: the sight of the creeper thriving by the wayside. Unmistakably a presentiment; why else should it be so vividly imprinted on his mind's eye, as though every bend would reveal its hidden glory?

He would have been annoyed had anyone dared call him superstitious. Yet, the truth was that he couldn't shake off a strong feeling that nature had singled him out, that she was indeed conspiring with him to divulge one of her lost secrets. Another reason for his optimism was a conviction he held—almost an article of faith—that no species of vegetation in evergreen or rain forests remained extinct for long. Using the instance of the *Passiflora boliviana*—which incidentally had been regarded by ancient tribes as a gift of the gods, having tremendous medicinal value for healing bone tissue—he hoped to develop his thesis that, in certain types of forest, when left alone by man, regeneration was a constant, cyclical reality. It wasn't a completely original idea, that's true—others like McCallum had mooted it in the past—but never had it been conclusively established.

Moreover, he felt it serendipitous that time should collude to assist his search for this 'extinct' or, as he preferred to believe, rare plant. For the entire next week school would remain officially closed. It was going to be 'prep' break, before the semester-end exams commenced; this interval, combined with a couple of consecutive public holidays gave him a whole ten days off for his field research. The kids had no classes to attend; they were supposed to spend this time in the study hall. He himself had no teaching duties during these ten days, except to make himself available to students if they required clarification in his subject.

In less than a month, after marking their answer-booklets, he would be free to go back to Delhi. Perhaps the birth of his child, coinciding with his own homecoming, would bring him good fortune. He hoped to hear from Colorado in the next week or two. He had already planned to support his preliminary application to the university with a précis of the research document he was drafting on the *Passiflora boliviana* . . . once supported by his find, of course, his specimen, which now, with galloping certainty, he felt was only a matter of days. He imagined that day in some detail, when he would carry it himself, carefully held between the leaves of a cloth folder to the famous Rapinat herbarium in Tiruchirapalli in the plains (he would have to set out early, having first made an appointment with the Jesuit pedagogues who ran the institute; on his motorcycle he'd get there in less than three hours). Rapinat was considered authoritative enough by scholars in his line of work. A certification from there would carry much weight, but just to be doubly and unequivocally acknowledged for his research, he would courier another sample to the Kew, in London.

There were moments of self-doubt, of course, when he wondered if all this was not mere fantasy. If his hopes of finding recognition and posting at a foreign university were not mere dreams to compensate for his loneliness, his domestic troubles, the imponderables over his unborn child. Well, life had taught him never to countenance failure. That was his credo, his impetus for living. If he could just keep a cool head, follow things through to their logical end . . .

So far, none of the students had asked Anand for extra help. Relishing the poise and self-possession his situation gave him,

Anand worked vigorously and joyfully to comb the forests he was surrounded by. Usually setting out before lunch, he would carry a few packed sandwiches, a flask of water, and a small digital camera. On a detailed map of the Palanis, he had superscribed his own sub-divisions with a fine marker, segments small enough to cover thoroughly in just one or two afternoons. In this planned and systematic manner, he explored sometimes large, sometimes minute portions of the hilly countryside every single day. In the evenings, he would score through the segments he was satisfied he had researched diligently enough.

The scope of his enterprise was dizzyingly audacious, he knew. So far, he had found nothing of the plant he was looking for. But the botanical wealth he had encountered during these expeditions filled him with a sense of promise rather than futility or frustration. Returning to his cottage after dark, tired and dusty, he would fish out the key to the front door from the mailbox in which Amma would have dropped it on her way out. After letting himself in, he often lit the woodstove. Once he'd got a blaze going, replenishing it every now and then with a stout log or two, he stretched himself on the settee before its comforting warmth. He placed his dinner, which Amma had prepared, on the top-plate of the iron woodstove, until he could hear it simmer. Sitting cross-legged, he ate slowly, ponderously . . .

Then, on the morning of the seventh day of prep, something extraordinary happened.

About to set out for school to put in his brief but obligatory appearance, very softly, as though from a great distance, Anand heard the familiar cry of the old beggar.

Could he have imagined it? He was feeling a bit out of sorts, that morning. Somehow, sleep had eluded him all of last night—too much excitement?—he had woken up with a heavy head, unrefreshed. Now, however, a ghost of a smile appeared on his face. For nearly a week, he realized, he hadn't been made aware of the beggar's invariable presence outside his garden gate. Ever since he had moved into this cottage, the man's noxious entity had become a dark, ubiquitous shadow that grew larger by the day, invading his mind and clouding his very existence. But this was amazing! The man had disappeared into thin air. Come to think of it, ever since that afternoon when he had yelled at him . . . Victory! Like a combatant who trounces a formidable adversary, for a moment, his mind celebrated: but no . . . oh no, was the blighter back again?

Well, so long as he stationed himself somewhere else, in less noisome proximity, he couldn't care less. Or perhaps the end of the tourist influx meant that the old goat spent most of his time in the relative warmth of his hut, enjoying a well-deserved rest . . . but wait—there it was again. No doubt about it, that was his voice, and that—the same despicable war cry of self-deprecation! How else to describe it?

Latching his garden gate firmly, Anand stepped out on the road.

But now all he could hear were birds, the breeze swishing in the branches, the scrunch of shoes—his own—on moist, broken tarmac; and above all, a vast silence, overlaid with sounds of the forest. He kept his eyes peeled for the old rascal, but he was nowhere to be seen.

Suddenly, on the narrow, twisting road, an open truck sped

past, veering dangerously close. He narrowly escaped being knocked down, actually feeling the truck's rear view mirror whiz past his right ear. The back of the truck, piled high with jagged chunks of stone and rock, he caught only a glimpse of, before it rumbled on, vanishing around a bend; his heart was still beating hard. He resolved to be more watchful of errant driving . . . Late at night, or in the small hours of morning one heard at times loud blasts from very far away . . . Not distant thunder—by no stretch of the imagination—but illegal quarrying, which was rampant in the Palanis, he was sure. Probably officials and bureaucrats were all in on it for a slice of the pie.

Now the road was deserted again . . . Just a few feet ahead at a sharp turn in the road he saw something that triggered off quite another stream of thought. On a brick wall preempting a sharp drop into the ravine, under the canopy of a huge silver birch, lay a monkey stretched out on his side: two other monkeys—friends, relations, lovers?—were picking lice from the down on his neck, his lower back, his rump. Every louse detected by one or other of the assistants was hurriedly slipped between the finder's chops; then chewed slowly and meticulously, a relish to reward the frowning absorption they devoted to their search.

A month or so ago, while killing time for some reason in the staff lounge, he had watched a program on Discovery Channel (the Hindi teacher was addicted to TV-gazing, he sat before it whenever he could) that spoke of new research that indicated some sort of neuropathic communication between members of bands of monkeys. So that the one hunting for the other's lice was motivated not so much by neighbourly altruism, as by an equally palpable itching along identical meridians on his own body! Extricating the louse thus brought relief to both parties. Could this really be? If so, it had extraordinary implications! So much synchrony and coherence in our world? Were all living creatures, in fact force fields, connected, and communicating by invisible magnetic and electrical impulses? That's what the programme had tried to imply. But even while watching it, he had remained unconvinced by the evidence it offered in support of the hypothesis.

And now just a little further on, he saw something else that quite dismayed and angered him: a whole row of metal hoardings had come up along the road—overnight, literally—nailed into the broad trunks of old and beautiful trees . . . The garishly colourful Tamil inscriptions were incomprehensible to him but what disturbed Anand was the fact that people still couldn't grasp a simple truth—that trees were alive! To impale them like this, for the pittance that the municipality must earn by permitting this callow form of advertising . . . appalling arboreal crucifixions!

Anand cared for trees, for the life of nature, in steady retreat everywhere against the onslaught of civilization. Walking slowly towards school, thinking about the threatened ecologies of remote places like this resort, all of a sudden he heard the beggar's lamenting cry for alms. No mistake about it . . . Yet, when he looked around, both up and down either side of the road, he failed to see the beggar anywhere . . . Just as well, he thought; out of sight, out of mind . . . Still, the voice that assaulted his senses, seemed to emanate from some place very close by.

What really *was* happening to him this morning? He sensed an odd disturbance. Lack of sleep had probably lent an edge of excitability to his mind which was swinging like a monkey, from branch to branch, refusing to be at ease. During that short walk of fifteen minutes from home to school, a hundred—no, thousand—images, thoughts, ideas, sensations, impressions, feelings—not to mention being nearly crushed under a lorry—had surged through his head; now suddenly that ebullience had evaporated. He felt entirely vacant, even slightly depressed. But there was that voice again—he heard it several times in succession—now bleating, now beseeching, now booming . . . where was it coming from? He knew today would be eventful, but in what way, exactly? And why was he feeling so low? He had a headache coming on.

At the school gate, he said to himself, I must try to feel less distracted, I *must* calm my mind. But he realized this was easier thought than done. Throughout the morning, at regular intervals, he was tormented by the old beggar's wheezy incantation, now whispering, now taunting, now pounding his ears. He seemed to be everywhere around, and always in close proximity. Even in the staff-room, while talking to a student about the cellular classification of plants, he had heard the voice at least half a dozen times! Bloody preposterous! How could he have got past security, and on to school campus? How had the bastard managed to sneak in? He would report the matter, see that the watchmen on duty were severely reprimanded. They might well be in cahoots with the beggar, having been promised a percentage of his earnings for free access to the school. Suddenly, Anand was consumed by an inordinate loathing for vagabonds, wastrels, ruffians, all the subalterns of the world. But even now that voice . . . it just wouldn't let up.

Though annoyance and rage had accumulated in him to bursting point, yet another self, another part of him remained detached, unconvinced. More clinically observant, it wasn't impressed by Anand's agitation, remaining hesitant, mystified. All this excitement, exultation, fury racing through his head was rather distressing . . . That other self simply disbelieved all this was actually happening . . . And uneasily, Anand—Anand himself, the no-nonsense rationalist, the scientist—was persuaded that something uncanny *was* going on, something strangely unreal . . . For the first time in his life, he felt his mind was refusing to stand by him; it was stuttering, dissembling, slipping . . . Come to think of it, if a sleepless night could cause a man so much mental grief . . . in that very instant an image flashed across his mind and drained the blood out of his head. He felt he might faint, lose consciousness, if he didn't find somewhere to sit. Was last night's dream regurgitating itself in his subconscious? No, in the first place he was pretty sure it hadn't been a dream at all! He remembered clearly what had disturbed his sleep in the night. Like a flashback in a movie, the evocation, retrieved now, was charged with the memory of strong emotion. Once again, it made his hackles rise.

Something had woken Anand from his sleep last night—he didn't know what. When he opened his eyes, he saw moonlight streaming in through the large window by his bed. For a brief but penetrating instant, he saw the beggar's face at the window. The man was grinning at him in a vile and sensual manner. His gaze was riveted directly at his supine, sleep-numbed body. It terrified him, as a child takes fright when he awakens with a start from a bad dream: but this had been no nightmare, he was sure. The beggar, or his apparition, lurking outside his window, had moreover grown in dimension; the frail, wrinkled man had swelled up. His face was podgy and menacing: that evil grin occupied the best part of his large bedside window. A sudden chilly draft swept through the room—as though the window had actually been forced open. Terror had dropped a curtain over his eyes, and Anand had responded by pulling the blanket over his face. Presently, he had drifted off to sleep again. When it was morning, he remembered nothing of the night's macabre vision. He had blotted out all memory of it—until now.

Anand felt ashamed of himself; but also relieved that no one else knew he was seeing things. Was he flipping his lid? And all because of a bullying, persistent mendicant? An entire morning had been plagued by the beggar's pervasive cry; and last night—he remembered the episode clearly now—why had he been transformed into such a coward, crushed by sheer funk over optical tricks played by moonlight outside his bedroom window? And if he had believed it was no illusion, why hadn't he flung open the window and confronted the intruder? *Was* there one at all—what made him prefer instead to hide under his blanket?

Anyway, the question still remained. What *had* happened to the beggar? Since that afternoon when he had yelled at him, the man had disappeared completely from sight. He was old and feeble, no doubt. Could he have gone and died? If indeed that was the case, was his restless spirit seeking revenge on him, on all those who denied him alms?

On the other hand, probably he wasn't dead at all; he might

only be ill. And this thought somehow made him feel more guilty . . . The blast of his anger had certainly unnerved the old man, but more than that, perhaps—could it have delivered such a blow to his decrepit immune system that he could no longer fend off the diseases and debilities of old age? He might well be lying in his hut, terminally ill, with no one to tend to him . . . Must find out where he lives, and pay him a visit. He could leave behind a tenner or two to make up for all the times he had flatly refused assistance, some fruit as well, perhaps—just seeing him alive, even if ailing, might get the old man out of his head.

Thus, by an extraordinary twist of events, Anand began to long for just one more meeting with the noisy beggar, who in the very recent past had inspired in him so much dudgeon. The cry for mercy, for alms rang again in his head.

ammah, ta-hee
pitchai podoongey . . .
saaput laachche
nalaar irkun vaangey . . .
ammah, ta-hee, ammaaah . . .

Not that his grasp of the language had increased in these few months. He still understood not a word of the phrases that were turning in his head. Perhaps it was only from having heard them repeated so often that they had become engraved on his brain. Yet, how incredible that his mind should actually be able to reproduce the precise sequence of the words—even if just phonetically—with their strange Tamil inflexions, discordant sing-song, their pathetic whine.

It was positively unnerving! If he could have dipped his hand in his pocket and brought up a few coins, he would have gladly handed them over, if only to buy silence. But the beggar wasn't around anymore to receive his alms . . . Only the cry, now muttering in his head, now resounding defiantly, now moaning with self-pity.

He felt a strong urge to whisper to himself the runic formula that had been looping endlessly in his head like a spell. It was an irrepressible urge . . . The student he had been talking to had clarified his difficulties and left, there was no one else in the staff-room . . . If he could only speak the incantation out aloud—spit it out, once for all—perhaps it would stop gnawing at his brain. In a husky, breathless voice, Anand heard himself uttering those words.

'ammah, ta-hee . . .
pitchai podoongey . . .
saaput laachche
nalaar irkun vaangey . . .
ammah, ta-hee, ammaaah . . .

He'd got it right from beginning to end! The whole damn caboodle, without scrambling a word. How ever had he learned it so well? His mind was in a whirl. What meaning could he ascribe to this insanity, this charade his subconscious mind had willy-nilly imposed on him? Was it, as in the case of the monkeys, a shared itch—excoriating his conscience for what he had done to the beggar? What had he done in fact? Okay, he *had* been very rough with him on that one occasion; at other times, too, he had scarcely concealed the contempt and disgust he felt . . . But then, on occasion, he had given him money, too, hadn't he?

It gave Anand much relief to realize that it wasn't so difficult, after all, to find an exit from the mental cul-de-sac he found himself in. So long as he was out-of-doors, away from school and town, making his exploratory botanical forays into the countryside, neither any thought of the beggar nor his creepy ululation impinged on him. It pleased him to note that while working, he was invariably more focused, content. The secret to a healthy mind was, he had always believed that, hadn't he—work. Whatever happens now, I have to continue my efforts of the last two weeks. Once he had found the matchless *Passiflora boliviana* he could resign his job, escape forever this gloomy, dank, overgrown paradise, with its perpetually overcast skies, its wildly profuse vegetation. Once he was back in Delhi with Pamela and his child, nothing would matter. For the very first time since taking up his teaching job in this remote, alien region of the country, he felt very lonely.

However, the next morning, Anand decided to plunge back into work. Now his excursions in pursuit of the passion flower were keenly serrated by an edge of feverish impatience. He didn't want the beggar question to oppress him anymore. Ignoring realistic odds, he tramped over hillsides, wading through muddy streams, entering unexplored natural grottoes, stark rocky caverns, sifting through leafy arbours . . . But alas, no *Passiflora boliviana* yet.

Overcome by depression, that night he genuinely began to wonder whether it was the prospect of failure that was unraveling his mind, stuffing it with Tamil gobbledygook to divert him from inevitable defeat?

(v)

All he had left now were three days before school resumed. To make matters worse, the weather had taken a nasty turn.

After more than a month of drought-like conditions, it had poured all night long. There was a lull in the downpour just now, but Anand knew it couldn't last. Meanwhile, everywhere the earth had turned slushy and squelchy.

During the last days of prep, five boys and a girl had discovered difficulties in his subject, and decided they needed extra help; fortunately, their areas of confusion overlapped somewhat, and Anand was able to address them all in a group. Even so, it was half past ten when he finished with them. The sky was layered with grey clouds.

But he wasn't going to waste a single moment. Immediately after a hot coffee, slipping into a rubberized 'Duckback' overcoat and a plastic hood, Anand set out for a part of the hills he hadn't explored thoroughly enough.

All through the afternoon, thunder rumbled softly, as though the grey blotch of sky were clearing its throat; frequently, a fork of lightning dissected the heavens; five hours later, on his way back into town, there wasn't much change in the weather. The rain had stopped, but at 3.45 in the afternoon, the dismal light foreshadowed late evening.

All in all it had been a difficult day that had yielded no results. A thick mist hung in the air making it difficult to see the road. He was still half an hour away from town when he saw another apparition: the old beggar standing in the middle of his path, wrapped in silvery fog. There were no human dwelling-places nearby; both sides of the road were fringed with thick forest.

The memory of the face that had so vividly appeared at his bedroom window two nights ago, made Anand rub his eyes in disgust. Another illusion? Nevertheless, as he drew nearer the figure, he felt himself turn cold. Poor visibility conditions compelled him to drive very slow. Even so, Anand felt brave enough to say to himself: once and for all I will ascertain if it really is the beggar standing there in flesh and blood or some shade from the underworld.

The figure saw him approach and began his characteristic bowing. An outstretched hand levered up and down mechanically. But oddly, there was no sound from him at all. If indeed it was the beggar, why was he performing these motions without calling for alms? Had he lost his voice? Did he have a sore throat?

Without a word, expressionless, Anand passed him by. Through a corner of his eye, he glimpsed that the old man was actually grinning at him in recognition. He didn't stop, or say anything to acknowledge the beggar's presence, refusing even to look directly at him. But once he had passed him by, he wished he had; he regretted so much not saying a word or smiling at him that he was tempted to turn his head and look back—if only to confirm that the figure hadn't dematerialized into mist the moment he had crossed his path. And indeed, what could that silent, gloating grin, so reminiscent of the nocturnal visitation, have meant? He realized, in retrospect, he had made a terrible mistake.

Immediately ahead was a sharp turn in the road. As his

attention snapped back to the road and he realized the danger he was in, he panicked, and his motorcycle skidded violently over slush. When he hit the ground, he lost consciousness, but before he did, Anand's final thought was: no question about it, the rascal is still very much alive. A ghost would never cover his head with a tatty, ochre plastic sheet . . .

(vi)

Dazed and broken, Anand harboured few hopes of surviving his ordeal. A great autumnal gale was blowing without respite, making the stoutest of trees shudder. In a large grove below where he lay, tall slender pines swayed and soughed. The night would be freezing cold—if he lasted through it, that is. This was one crisis he had no chance of simply walking away from. At least not without serious assistance. And hardly anyone would discover him here, even by accident. In all probability, he'd never see Pamela again; or their soon-to-be-born infant child.

His hands, his face, every exposed part of his body was severely pricked and scratched and stabbed by thorns and branches that he had crashed through during his fall. Yet, these were but minor abrasions compared to the excruciating pain in his left leg that penetrated his entire being; unable to bear the pain Anand blacked out

When he came to again, it had grown pitch dark. He tried to tell the time by staring at the luminous dial of his wristwatch, only to remember it had smashed during the fall, its hands frozen at six thirty-five.

And then incredibly, even as he shivered with cold and was

wracked with pain he felt renewed. It was as though he were witnessing a miracle—through the dense lattice of vegetation he saw a glimmer of light, heralding the approaching dawn. He had survived the night. No wild cat or hyena had dragged him into the brush. The dark clouds in the sky had almost completely cleared up. A few clusters of stars still shone, dimly.

Very gradually, in the distance, a range of hills appeared: so faint and far away, he couldn't be sure he wasn't imagining them; from what he could make out, they were exquisite. Bit by bit, acquiring presence, filling up with details of light and shade, shape and texture . . . brushstroke upon brushstroke, it seemed to him they were being moulded anew . . . There was nothing he could do, nothing he wanted to do, but lie there and watch, transfixed.

His mouth was dry. He hadn't had anything to eat or drink in maybe twenty hours. He tried to ease his body a little by shifting, but the pain that the slightest movement brought on was unbearable. He soon gave up the idea. The clump of shrubbery he had landed in—cow cockle if anything; at least that's what it looked like in this light, with those pale rose flowers—cradled him about as comfortably as he could have hoped to be . . . but the pain . . . agonizing. He had broken a bone; his tibia, or was it called fibula?

Now the sun appeared above those sublimely proportioned hills, its limpid glow gradually illuminating the million shades of green that Anand was cosseted by. The innumerable shapes and forms of leaf and branch—each almost identical to the next, yet ever so slightly and subtly different—created a near-infinite network of dense canopies mounting above and beyond

Anand's dazed vision; out of these vast green distances shimmering with the delicate texture of life, at irregular intervals rose clumps of slender, budding trees, offerings to the cool mountain air . . . The gentle warmth of the sun had awoken in Anand's body an appetite to go on living . . . all was not lost, not yet. Suddenly he felt unbearably hungry. Looking around him, he reminded himself that most plants were edible.

Just a few feet behind him lay the second-hand Royal Enfield he had purchased at the auto spare parts shop in the township market, its front wheel twisted. But what interested Anand more than the wreckage of his motorbike, were some mushrooms sprouting from the exposed root of a large oak; if he stretched his body upwards he might just reach them.

Stretching cautiously, in anticipation of a blast of nerve-wracking pain, Anand uprooted a handful. They were very tender. A scholarly voice hemmed and hawed in his head, reminding him that mushrooms could be poisonous, or sometimes hallucinogenic. But another voice, gentler and more timid, whispered, 'You need to eat to keep going. Eat us, we'll do you good . . .'

As the spectacle of creation awakened before his eyes, Anand chewed on the mushrooms. They tasted very good. He ate slowly, savouring every morsel. Patterns of light seeped through countless leaf-cluster formations illuminating their outlines in relief, highlighting and darkening their masses to create a multi-dimensionality beyond geometry. It was like a grand display of silently transmuting fireworks. Branches, too, some swollen, bulbous and mossy, others meagre and wraith-like, snaked sinuously towards a glittering sky . . . His tongue felt parched and swollen; but his eyes were streaming . . . His face was moist with tears. He was crying with pity for himself, for never having loved the world enough, for never having appreciated or understood its great beauty and meaning; its great coherence. He had placed *himself* above everything else, always at its centre; or apex, rather, from where he could look down and control . . .

Well, what had it all come to, finally? The desire to be distinctive and special, to believe he was several notches above the rest. The great hunger for fame and fortune, the ambition to be acknowledged as better than the best, with a research chair to his name at a foreign university, the impassioned but psychopathic quest for *Passiflora boliviana* that was to have resulted in all these? Had it all been worth it? Below that obsessive hunt for the flower lurked another weakness, one he could never bring himself to admit to: simple greed. He had managed to mask it completely, even from himself, by becoming so venomously critical of a poor beggar. It was not the beggar who was greedy and manipulative. The hatred Anand felt for him, or had thought he felt for him, was not inspired by the beggar, but by the mirror the old man was holding up to him, in which Anand caught a glimpse of his own self.

Suddenly the light began to change, a brooding, gradual shift as happens during a solar eclipse. Soon, everything was awash with a velvety softness, a fluidity coloured with the kindness of love.

And Anand became a baby, an infant lying upon the crib of the earth. He was still the same Anand, but now he had become aware of the power of the place that cradled him, as an infant is aware of its mother's heartbeat. He felt its throb in his blood as it gushed through his veins and flowed to every sense organ . . . Everything and all of this was alive. He knew this not as an abstract notion, but as palpably, overwhelmingly true. He could feel the world breathing, the rocks, the lichen, the quivering blades of grass, the limbs and twigs and flowers and birds, all, all of it was alive.

'You don't need to prove yourself to anyone, Anand.'

Suddenly, apropos of nothing, he heard Pamela's husky voice.

'Least of all to me . . . We can be happy with less. At least, you and me, we'll always be there for each other, won't we?'

That kind of love-talk had always made him squirm. He never liked making blanket promises, always shied away from verbalizing commitment. But now, he felt differently. He was consumed by great regret for never having loved anyone or anything whole-heartedly, not even Pamela. He wanted to proclaim his love for her aloud. Anand swore that if he should have just one more chance, he would never again live so selfishly as he had in the past. Something was going on . . . what was it? Something was happening to him. Was it the effect of the mushrooms?

The churning in his brain had clapped a strange device onto his inner eye, which allowed him to regard himself with fierce clarity . . . Anand Mahendroo. Neither blissful, nor joyous, the name his mother had chosen for him some thirty-odd years ago had proved a complete misnomer. In all those years he hadn't lived up to the meaning of his name in any way. Rather he had been angry, irascible, contemptuous, selfish, cunning, manipulative and only interested in executing the plans he had drawn up in his own head. But what kind of a life had it been? One that he now considered barely worth having lived. Yes, he had lived despicably.

He had no memory of his father, almost none. In those possibly terminal moments of his life, Anand's thoughts searched out the strong clean-shaven features of a uniformed soldier, whose black-and-white framed photograph hung on the living-room wall of his Delhi apartment. A colonel in the Indian army, he had seen action during the Bangladesh war and perished in it before Anand turned four. His body was never found. Yet, though there were no real memories, somehow Anand remembered his father as a kind man. In his absence, Mother had raised him single-handedly; but with greater military zeal, he knew, than his father would ever have wanted to impose on his only child . . . While he was a toddler, his mother had found his fascination with flowers offensive, perhaps it embarrassed her because it made him out to bc a trifle effeminate. In the park one evening, she had rebuked him for kissing the soft petals of a pink rose.

'Don't ever do that, Anand-beta, please,' she had said, ominously. 'Next time, a worm could wriggle up your nose. And then that worm will live in your brain, eating it up, bit by bit. No smelling flowers again, do you hear me?'

Despite that alarmist threat, the seed of an enduring fascination with plants and flowers had germinated with time.

And now, time had reached a stasis. Minutes, even hours could have passed without his being aware of them. His watch was broken, and the magically luminous light, continually refracting through verdure, refused to betray the hour. Not that he cared any more what time it was. His hunger had subsided; he felt hardly any pain in his leg. Here he was, a botanist, lying wounded in the lap of luxuriant greenery, surrounded by brushwood and scrub and gorse, by heather and furze, and all manner of plants and trees and creepers. But, alas, no *Passiflora boliviana* . . . An orange butterfly, its wings streaked with purple, landed for a moment on his fractured leg, then disappeared. It had stopped there for only an instant, yet in its weightless touch, Anand felt much solace.

Then a breeze caressed his face, and for no reason, he found himself suddenly laughing. He felt like a baby again. And once more, he heard the warm husky voice of his beloved, Pamela: 'Where are you, Anand? You must come home quickly, see what a beautiful, perfect baby has been born to us . . . You didn't believe in God when I told you you should . . . But now, Jesus be praised, believe, Anand, believe . . . when you see our baby, you will believe . . .' And Anand's own laughter gurgled and reverberated through the woods.

All of a sudden, he became aware of footsteps, a crunching of leaves and twigs, hurrying towards where he lay. He craned his neck and looked towards the sound. He should have felt great relief that a rescue party had found its way to him at last. But when he saw the two men whose heavy footfalls were tramping towards him, he felt afraid. The one who was leading the way looked exactly like the old beggar—only thirty years younger! It was amazing . . . the podgy face staring at him through his bedroom window! It made his hair stand on end . . . Muscular and dark and not bespectacled, but the similarity in bone structure, face and every muscle, even skin tone matched the old man's so completely, it took his breath away. It was as if the old beggar had quaffed some elixir of youth and come down now, almost a whole day after the accident he would have surely witnessed, to exact his revenge in the silence of the woods. The youthful beggar was accompanied by another man, also dressed in a vest and lungi, equally swarthy and menacing.

But they didn't stop near where he lay. Almost without noticing him at all, they stomped past, further into the ravine, tunneling through thick undergrowth towards the grove of tall conifers, until they couldn't be seen at all. Anand felt let down. He wondered if he should have yelled, or spoken up, drawn attention to his injury, asked for help. Might they disappear without offering assistance? He began to scream for help. But his throat was dry, and his voice hardly carried.

Presently, the two men returned, climbing upward jauntily. At first Anand saw only their heads bobbing above the brush, then their torsos, then the rest of them. And then he saw what they were carrying in their hands. He almost yelled out in consternation as a muddle of emotions went tripping through his brain—joy, surprise, outrage and hurt—for both men were carrying in each hand bunches of rudely ripped-up and twisted remnants of a creeper he recognized immediately: *Passiflora boliviana*!

'Hey, give me that,' croaked Anand, his throat hardly able to articulate the words. 'Where did you find that?'

But the language problem was not so easily overidden. Both men had heard him speak, but their expressions remained blank. Now, looking at the passion flower creeper from a distance of perhaps four feet, Anand was surer than before that that's what it was. He got more excited.

'Just give me that plant,' he raised his voice, peremptorily. In his mind's eye a picture flashed of his small digital camera, probably lying smashed near the site of the accident. This was a miracle, but he needed to record it for posterity! For the guys in Colorado!

'What are you doing?' he called out again, more agitated than before. One of the men signaled him to be quiet. And then the duo proceeded, as if by pre-planned agreement, to shred the plants they were carrying into smaller bits, stuffing them carelessly into a small plastic carry-bag.

'What're you doing? Stop!' cried Anand in horror. 'I need that plant! You are destroying something very precious. Give me that!' But there was no comprehension at all on the part of the other two. It was clear they were humouring him as they might a raving lunatic; gesturing to him every now and then to remain calm. Presently, one of the men unfolded a large quilted blanket and spread it out on the ground beside Anand. Then the stronger of the two gripped him by his shoulders, and the other took his feet. Anand screamed in pain as they raised him and put him on the blanket. But it was fear that multiplied his pain a hundredfold. Who *were* these men? Where were they taking him? Had the old beggar found out somehow the enormous significance the *Passiflora boliviana* had for him? Was that why he had sent his henchmen to destroy every last specimen of the creeper? What a revenge that bastard was exacting: to have them rip to shreds what he had been so desperately seeking all these weeks in front of his very eyes? And now, was he about to enact the next part of his diabolical plan? What was it going to be? Where were they taking him? He would resist.

And so he did. As they lifted Anand up in the blanket, he yelled and screamed, twisted and lunged hysterically at his abductors . . . It never occurred to Anand that they might be trying to help. They could hardly have been blamed if in the course of the feeble but frantic resistance he put up, his fractured limb knocked against a random tree trunk. A shriek of pain rang through those hills. After that, Anand struggled no more.

(vii)

When he awoke, Anand did not recognize his surroundings at all. But he was not cold.

A warm blanket was laid over him. Oddly, he felt no pain, though his leg felt as though it had turned to stone.

He lifted up the musty-smelling blanket that covered him and peered inside. Someone had skillfully bandaged his right leg with a strip of cloth, after smearing it with some gluey brown paste. To keep the broken bone from shifting, both sides were buttressed with sacks of wet mud. Yes, the pain was nearly gone, and the swelling at his knee, that too had mostly subsided. The truth flashed on Anand in a moment of great exhilaration: those men in the forest had been so careless with the plants they were collecting because they knew all along they would have to be ground into the balm that coated his fractured leg. It was true then, the legendary healing powers of the *Passiflora boliviana* . . .! It was a miracle that his suffering should be so quickly relieved, and by the agency of the very plant he had spent so much time and energy trying to find.

Anand looked around, but couldn't see very much. He was lying on a wooden string cot in the outer courtyard of a small stone-and-mud house. After a while, a very bony, old woman draped in a dark sari appeared. Perhaps she had come out only to check if he was awake. Their eyes met, but she offered no smile or words of greeting. She went back inside immediately, wearing a tired and mournful expression.

Then the old beggar himself appeared, and Anand was excited to see him. Ever since he had regained consciousness, Anand had had a hunch that these were the old man's lodgings and, of course, the young men who had brought him here his sons.

An appreciative and grateful smile began to appear on Anand's face, but the old man only scowled, and ignored him. Then the beggar's look-alike son came out, and bent down respectfully to touch his father's feet. The beggar placed a hand on his son's head and muttered what may have been a benediction. For a few minutes, both father and son went inside the house and Anand could hear what sounded like softly intoned Sanskrit shlokas. How could he thank these men for having saved his life? What a strange turn of events that he should be granted this privilege of seeing the old man's home, of meeting his family . . .

Did the old beggar actually walk a good forty-five minutes or an hour every day to get to his begging-post near Suicide Point? What work did his sons do, and how much did the family earn collectively? It was obviously a poor household, but they seemed to own some livestock—Anand had heard a rooster crowing earlier that morning—and ran a reasonable establishment.

These were the thoughts and questions that passed through Anand's head as he lay there on the cot observing everything. He hadn't been entirely wrong then, in suspecting the beggar of being a hustler! He felt a certain amount of satisfaction as he realized this. But perhaps the continual badgering of tourists for money was the only kind of work he could undertake at his age, which lent itself admirably to such an occupation, and perhaps the only kind he could find in this underdeveloped hill region.

As the morning advanced, a sense of normalcy descended on Anand. He was not anxious any more. It was lucky that the old man had witnessed his accident, for he knew well that Anand worked at L'Ecole Internationale, and would know whom to get in touch with. It was odd that nobody from the school had turned up yet, and had left him to the mercy of the old man and his sons! Somehow, in spite of the revelatory nature of his experiences of the previous day, in spite of his incipient awareness of the oneness of the world and all living things, in spite of all that he had to be grateful to the old man for, he found that he still disliked the scoundrel as much as he always had. He was sorry that he felt as he did, but the feeling persisted in his gut.

The old woman came out again with a cup of warm, slightly watery, sweetened milk. She seemed nicer than the others. Anand drained the cup, savouring the warmth of the milk. It tasted good. Fleetingly, he remembered his recent desire to locate the missing beggar and give him some money to make peace. A passing thought occurred to him now—how much should he give the old man for his assistance. He felt for his wallet. It was still in his trouser pocket. How much would he feel satisfied with for the night's hospitality? A hundred? He should be reasonably happy with that. Or maybe he should make that two hundred. From behind the house a white goat flecked with black patches wandered out and climbed the steps that lead to the porch; he eyed Anand sternly, as though wondering if it made sense to butt a supine man; then he wandered back down the steps and went away. The other members of the household, too, were nowhere to be seen.

Anand didn't have to wait long before a car drove up and stopped outside the beggar's courtyard. Presently, he saw Banerji's stick, and then Banerji himself emerge from the car. The school's ambulance, too, drove up behind him.

'Ah, there you are, Mahendroo,' he said, approaching Anand's cot. 'I told you to be careful, didn't I? It's treacherous terrain . . . Anyway, thank God you're safe . . . We were very worried, of course. And if it wasn't for Muthusamy here, we might never have found you . . .' He conversed with the old man in effusive Tamil for a few minutes. They seemed to be exchanging notes on what had transpired the previous day.

'Such bad weather these past two days, Mahendroo. That's what made the task of rescue so much more difficult. We had nearly given up on you, until—' said Banerji, gesturing towards the old man. 'You certainly owe him a lot.' Apparently the old man had gone to the school the previous evening to inform Banerji of the accident, while his sons, at his direction, were already carrying him out of the ravine on the blanket.

'As soon as you're ready, we'll shift you to the school dispensary, where you'll get modern treatment from Dr Roy, the school doctor. Who's also a qualified surgeon, incidentally,' said Banerji. 'Your benefactor here has tried some herbal mumbo-jumbo on you, he told me about it quite proudly just now; though I dare say you look none the worse for it. Oh, but before I forget: I have to give you an urgent message. Your wife has been phoning from Goa, three times since yesterday. She wants you to call her back as soon as you can . . . I didn't tell her about your accident, of course. She appeared to have enough worries as it is—'

A slow smile spread on Anand's face. He was beaming with pride as he interrupted Banerji, 'No, no worries. I was expecting her to call . . . She would have phoned about our baby which she was expecting any day .'

Banerji frowned, then shrugged. 'Could be. But she did sound a bit tense . . . Please call her back soon as we get to school . . .'

'Of course, I can't wait to . . . Though I'm very sure she phoned to give me the news about our baby . . . Our baby's been born on time, as expected.'

'I may be completely wrong, of course . . . Shall I ask the driver to bring out the stretcher?'

Anand felt a sudden rush of anger against the VP. What the hell was the old fool on about? Of course you're wrong, you pompous ass. Of course, Pamela wanted to tell me about the baby . . . It's not something one leaves a message about with a total stranger. And the baby was . . . is fine, of course. Everything's fine.

Finally, as much as he disliked asking Banerji to serve as interpreter for him, he still had some important, unfinished business here. He appealed to Banerji to ask Muthusamy and his sons a question on his behalf.

'Would you please ask if they can get me a few more of those plants which they used on my leg?' Anand queried, and Banerji translated for him. Their answer went on and on. The old man and his sons spoke endlessly, interrupting one another, elaborating, presumably, on each other's depositions, while Anand waited anxiously trying hard to grasp what was being said. Finally, after almost five minutes, Banerji provided him with the gist of their answer.

'They crushed every last specimen they could find, they say, to prepare sufficient quantities of the balm. Unfortunately . . .' explained Banerji, shaking his head. 'It's a very rare plant, they tell me, one that flowers only once in twelve years! And even when it does appear, they said, the blossoms last for only twenty-four hours, then wither and die . . . Can you believe it, Mahendroo? You're a very lucky man! Once in twelve years, and then only for twenty-four hours!'

For some inexplicable reason, Banerji found all this very funny. Then he said something in Tamil to the others, and Muthusamy and his sons laughed uncontrollably. Were they laughing at him?

'What's so funny?' asked Anand.

'An old Tamil proverb that came to mind . . . how do I translate it? It's almost impossible to render into English—nadyavattam shankavalli mookarattai tezhudaamanattam . . . These are names of mythical plants from our scriptures . . .

supposed to have been used by monks and novices to aid enlightenment. I suppose, very roughly you could say—a single sprig of manna in the palm of your hand equals ten thousand in the imagination; though the imagination is so much more overgrown with miracles. . . . Of course, I'm mixing my idioms and metaphors . . . just to give you a sense of the phrase . . .' Banerji couldn't stop chuckling, but Anand failed to understand the proverb, or see what was so amusing about it at all. Finally, the VP said, 'Come, are you ready?'

The driver of the ambulance, along with an attendant, was waiting beside Anand's cot with a stretcher.

'They'll lift you up and move you . . . This may hurt a bit . . . aah . . . slowly . . . don't worry, they're professionals . . . Easy now . . . Slowly . . . We don't want to cause Sir any more pain than necessary . . .'

Bokha

Bokha. It means 'toothless'. That's what everyone called him.

The name was a slight exaggeration. Only four of his front teeth were missing—two upper canines, two lower incisors—but the ones that remained were long, misshapen and tar-stained. And one corner of the ungainly assortment sported an inordinately large gold pre-molar, installed not many years ago, when Bokha had had a lucky streak at the cotton figures—glinting dully every time his face spread itself in that ugly leering grin that had earned him his nickname.

Bokha was known to be a deceitful, spiteful, untrustworthy, ridiculous sort of fellow. A petty swindler and, when occasion allowed, usually only with children, a wicked bully. His real name was Rutton Ollia, though few knew him by it. Short and rather puny, Bokha was getting on in years. His unshaven stubble and sparse hair were liberally sprinkled with grey, his clothes were old and baggy, and he had a comical manner of walking—especially, if he was in a hurry—when all his limbs appeared to be whirling about him in two or three tangential directions like the blades of a complex propeller. He was never seen without the greasy, black skull-cap poised at the slightly pointed end of a large cranium. Most people were abominably rude to him, and pushed him around.

Worst of all, he was himself completely craven and obsequious. There were no limits to the amount of self-humiliation he could undertake just to bum a cigarette or a drink off someone. He clowned, spat, cursed foully, made obscene gestures and gross noises while grovelling before his tormentors, merely to earn their derisive laughter, or their blows. People despised Bokha; but the truth was, he despised them a hundred times more. He derived a queer satisfaction from having his long nose tweaked, or from slurping up a spilt drink like a cat from the sun mica-topped tables in the bar at the instigation of his enemies and his patrons. It was proof to him that they were animals of the worst sort, beasts, lower than himself.

Usually, for a few hours every morning, Bokha worked as delivery boy at the local fire temple. That is to say, balancing the big, round, silver-plated trays of sanctified fruit knotted together in a white sheet, he carried them on his head to the homes of those who had ordered prayers for their dead that day. Eruchsaa, the head priest at the temple, was a burly, bearded old man who, though otherwise gentle and soft-spoken, became extraordinarily infuriated by the mere sight of Bokha, whom he considered sly and lazy.

'Donkey! Ghelo! Gadhero!' the old priest's deep voice would bellow in the vault-like back chambers of the fire temple, if some trays were lying uncleared or, simply, for no apparent reason. 'Where are your brains? In your arse? You lazy, good-for-nothing, bloody Bokha!' Frequently the priest would give Bokha a hard rap with the flat of his palm and send his cap flying. On perceiving Bokha bare-headed, Eruchsaa would become even more incensed.

'Put it on! Put it on! Shameless! You naked, toothless beggar!' he'd splutter, and start pummeling him with blows. (For it was forbidden to be without a cap in the temple precincts.)

Though there would appear not to be anything so offensive or demeaning about a nickname like 'toothless', there was something in the way it was spat out by people—by everyone who addressed him—'Aae Bokha!'—that stung him deeply and made his hackles rise. But his anger was a strange, dislocated thing which had no bearing on the world of people; when shouted at, Bokha's own voice turned shrill and his knees trembled with an inexplicable fear too powerful to control.

'No, no, Eruchsaa! What did I do?' he would cry, dancing around the old priest, avoiding his fists. 'Beat me! Beat me more! I am yours. I have eaten your salt, now I'll eat your blows as well . . .'

Then Bokha would suddenly pretend to be frantically busy, rushing this way and that, stomping his feet as though impatient of his own slowness, make motions in the air, polish a table here for a brief second, shift a vase there, stop to kiss the feet of the Prophet every time he passed the large heavily-garlanded painting on glass that reflected the flickering of oil-lamps lit by devotees in the temple's main hall. Oddly enough, this furious activity would placate Eruchsaa, who would leave him alone for the rest of the morning.

In the evening, Bokha could always be found in the crowded country liquor bar at the end of Forjett Road. Here, he earned his drinks working as bar help for the one-eyed Irani, Gustasp, mopping tables, collecting and rinsing out empty glasses and providing general entertainment to the sadistic impulses of the regulars, who knew him well. He stayed till closing time, then trudged home, drunk, swaying reluctantly in the direction of his small dark apartment.

What if I don't go home? thought Bokha one night. Couldn't I just stretch out here beside that one . . . Forget I have a bed and mattress, never enter that lane again, or see that house . . .?

Bokha gazed at the row of pavement sleepers with envy. Supine in the warmth of the night, some embracing, limbs entangled in a daze of sleep, he longed to be one of them. Sometimes, during the day, when he glimpsed one of the old chaps from school, smartly decked out with tie and shoes and briefcase, he felt the same kind of longing. Mostly, those schoolmates never recognized him . . . But no, here he was already. Too late to change anything now. In her bed, upstairs, his mother was lying awake waiting for him to return, so she could piss.

~

Those who had seen Bokha grow up placed the blame for his wretchedness squarely on his mother, the savage and formidable Khorshedmai. His father had died when he was only nine. Apoplexy, the doctor said. Something burst in his brain. And then she came into her own, this Khorshedmai. How she bloated! Lay in bed and ate and ate, while the boy ran completely wild. She showed more concern for stray alley-cats, whom she fed saucersful of milk, people said, than she ever did for her own son. Yet, every now and then, she would rouse from her apathy, as from a dream, and brutally punish the boy for some reported misdemeanor. Then, late in the night, the tortured child's screams of pain would rack the neighbourhood. No one dared interfere. They remembered these things, some of the neighbours, and were moved to pity for that spineless, unhappy loafer without an iota of self-respect, that Bokha.

She was definitely a bad sort. On the very morning after her husband's funeral, Khorshedmai quarreled violently with other tenants in her building over a small matter of uncleared garbage. Some of her neighbours had the careless habit of tipping their refuse in a back lot behind the building. But that wasn't all. She turned away Jimmy's relations and friends at the door when they came to condole. She even physically assaulted his best friend, Behram, nearly knocking him down the stairs when he showed a little persistence in trying to gain entry into his dead friend's flat.

On the fifth day, after services for the dead man were done, Khorshedmai came out onto the balcony of her third floor flat and began to beat her breast, beseeching God to bear witness to her sorrows. It was an extraordinary performance. She raised her head high, howled and shrieked, cursing her deceased husband to high heaven for abandoning her so thoughtlessly, without a paisa to her name, and a little one to tend for . . .

'O you cowardly wretch! Spendthrift, villainous rake! How could you trick me so, going off and dying like that, weakling . . .!'

Jimmy Ollia was respected in the neighbourhood, not least for the dignity with which he had borne his wife's shenanigans.

His friends knew of a handsome insurance policy he had made out in Khorshedmai's name, on which he had regularly paid the premiums. Nevertheless, Khorshedmai began to live in extreme poverty, like a miser. She pulled her son out of school and let him take to the streets.

It was then people began to say that though Jimmy Ollia had probably died in fit of rage against his wife's laziness and gluttony, who was to say she hadn't slipped something into his food? They would lower their voices when they spoke of Khorshedmai—if they spoke at all. It was rumoured that she had more than just a smattering of knowledge of the black arts. Someone remembered an apocryphal story about a good-looking young servant boy from a nearby building whom Khorshedmai took a fancy to even while Jimmy was still alive. That boy had been caught by the watchman of the cemetery behind the hill one night, just as he was digging up a freshly buried corpse! That was years ago. But it was commonly assumed that the servant had been a mere pawn in some evil design of hers. Overnight, the boy's hair had turned white and he had become completely deranged.

For three years, Khorshedmai let her son loaf. Then one day she spoke to a priest at the fire temple and arranged a job for him as a chasniwalla, a delivery boy. As for herself, she put on enormous amounts of weight. Day by day, week by week, she grew more obese until her ungainly masses of fat made her a sight to behold. Which was rare. She never left the house and was only glimpsed sometimes sitting at her window, impassive as a monument—a swollen old woman who was practically bedridden because her own corpulence had become too much for her to carry about. Otherwise, even at seventy, she was strong as a horse.

~

Bokha turned his key in the night-latch and entered silently. The gross silhouette of his mother's mound-like figure stretched out in bed on the other side of his own narrow cot by the window was etched into the darkness. She was snoring. Probably pretending to be asleep, thought Bokha. Waiting for me to lie down. Sure enough, as soon as he had crept into bed, he heard her powerful bass croak,

'Bedpan *aap*.'

She raised her body a few inches, and he shoved the bedpan under her. He turned his face away; the long, metallic ringing that followed, like the sustained peal of an electric buzzer, filled his ears with disgust.

'So much wakefulness,' Khorshedmai mumbled. 'I lie in bed and wait and wait. Where were you? So late?'

Her voice had a taunt hidden in it somewhere, like a splinter in a block of wood. He knew better than to answer. Khorshedmai kept vigil for him not merely to relieve her distended bladder, but also to engage in nocturnal altercation.

'With *her* I suppose . . . your ayah . . . Yes? Yes or no?' she pursued, as the ringing trickled to a halt. 'Take it out. Carefully now!'

Bokha did not need to be warned. Two nights ago he had come back tipsy and the bedpan, just as he had finished extricating it from under her, somehow tilted. Her thigh and mattress were splashed by urine. The suddenness of it all had caught Bokha off guard. He'd giggled. As soon as he had laid the pan on the floor, she had grabbed him by the arm and given him a sound thrashing. His ears still felt tender from the slaps she had showered on him. Once she had a grip on you, it was impossible to break loose. But so long as you remembered to stay outside her reach, you were all right because it was laughable to think of her pursuing anyone. The thought of his mother's restricted mobility amused Bokha, although it did not decrease the terror he held her in.

'Empty it out first,' his mother ordered.

But Bokha covered it with an old newspaper and hurriedly collapsed into bed.

'Tomorrow, in the morning,' he yawned and pretended to fall asleep instantly.

She cursed under her breath. For a few moments there was silence, punctuated by his mother's heavy breathing. Then she spoke again:

'Well, what do you do when you meet that ayah of yours . . .? Behind the bushes in the park? Do you stick your little finger in her? Or does she make you lick her black arse?' Khorshedmai laughed contemptuously. 'Poor boy, thirty-five and he's met his first girlfriend . . . a Catholic ayah, half-crazed like himself. I know everything that goes on, son. Sitting here, I get all the news . . .

'Well, take her at least, if you can,' her teasing flared and became a choking contempt. 'Can you? Eunuch! Or is your father's strain too strong in you, Bokha? My teeth are still good for cracking walnuts. Aae Bokha, why don't you answer?'

Bokha feigned a snore or two and lay very still. The moon had risen high, and its cold pallor bathed the room. He waited. At last he recognized a soft purring sound which told him his mother was really asleep. But Bokha was uncomfortable. An attack of gas was stirring biliously inside him. He had had nothing to eat all evening except peanuts and papad and stuff like that which people passed around while drinking.

Oh Lord, my ayah . . . Bokha smiled, despite himself. Seraphina . . . What a beautiful name. Not half so beautiful to look at, is she? And I don't know her quite so well as my jealous mother thinks I do. But I'll get to . . . I'll get to, you can be sure . . .

It pleased Bokha to realize that his mother's contemptuous raving only thinly disguised her anger, her fear . . . Fear of what? They had met two or three times in the municipal park where neighbourhood ayahs brought their little rich wards to while away the evening hours before it grew dark. Like a child she was herself, that Seraphina. Quite stupid, in fact . . . People said that once, many years ago, she had been possessed by an evil spirit who had ravished her every night; then, perhaps, tiring of her body, he had vacated it, but not without leaving his claw-marks on her soul. She was a duffer really, his Seraphina . . . But no matter what anyone said, she was kind to him.

She had been kind to him, to Bokha. Maybe he should just take over the evil spirit's place now. Bokha chuckled silently with lustful longing. But he would be a good spirit, of course. He would give her good times. He would do to her all those things his mad mother imagined he was doing. Seraphina. O Seraphina . . . Her name reminded him of the shape of a swan's back. The swan floated in his mind on a lake of alcohol. Its undulating sibilants soothed his besotted brain. Now he was caressing the swan. In the last moment before he reached his ecstasy, a cunning and triumphant thought reared its head and gloated: what if I really marry her, thought Bokha. Quite an ugly thing she is; but maybe I *will.*

(ii)

My father has left us and gone to a better world. That is how they put it. But I know he is dead. I felt the ice of his cheek on my lips when I kissed him. I held his hand and even shook it, but he would not respond. When they carried him up the hill to the Tower of Silence, I knew I would never see him again. What's more, Mummy knows it too. But when I'm around she still tries to hide her tears and speaks of my father as if he had left us for only a few days. Where is that better world? I believe Uncle Framroze knows something about it, because he has been trying to make contact with the dead. But first I must tell you how I came to be living with him.

A few days after my father passed on, his ex-employer offered my mother a job. Mother explained to me that she would have to start working, that she would be busy all day. Since my summer holidays had just begun, it was decided that I would spend them with Uncle Framroze. Even so, when the day came for me to go, I made a terrific fuss. Until Uncle said, 'Oh come now, I thought you were a grown-up boy. Why, I've even brought my car along, just to let you drive it.' That put things in a different light. I climbed into the funny-looking old car, called a Hillman. The suitcase Mummy had packed for me was in the back seat. I was in front, driving. Well, almost. Uncle allowed me to hold the wheel, and I'd honk loudly every time someone got in our way.

We drove slowly, carefully, up the steep road right to its farthest extreme where an oddly shaped, two-storeyed bungalow nestled against the side of Forjett Hill. A sheer rock face rose dark behind the house and loomed over it. 'Happy Home.' That's what it was called. It was to be my home for the next three months.

I grew to love the place. I loved it for its many rooms, so still and cool and dark, its dusty, secluded corners which had not been disturbed in years. For the long central corridor curling into the back of the house where a purplish-blue night lamp glowed day and night. For Pestonjee, who hung in this passage, my uncle's grey, red-cheeked, white-crested cockatoo who was eighty-three years old, but still whistling as merrily as a schoolboy. During the day, he would leave his cage and walk around the outside of its bars and climb the chain by which it was suspended. But in the evening he would return inside and sit gloomily on his perch, in a kind of huff of puffed-up feathers. I loved feeding Pestonjee. Green chillis, guavas, nuts. But what I loved most about that house were the high beams of its sloping, tiled roof which met in my room, directly above my bed. At the highest point, in a cavity created by the conjunction of two beams, sparrows had built and abandoned a nest. I stared at the roof every night for what must have been hours before I fell asleep.

Uncle was much older than my mother. He was a retired civil engineer who had remained a bachelor all his life. A kind, shy man, who was often embarrassed for not knowing what to say to me. Most of the time he would stay shut up in his room with his books and pamphlets and come out only for meals. His study-cum-prayer room fascinated me greatly. An entire wall had been converted into an altar and was covered with picture-frames of saints and sages, mystics, prophets and miracle-workers before whom he burnt large amounts of incense. My greatest pleasure during those days was to get him to tell me each one's story

Every Sunday morning, at ten o'clock sharp, my uncle would be visited by his three friends. They would drive up in an old DeSoto, honking loudly while they parked to announce their arrival. Bapsymai, Fardoon and Ghauswalla. These were their names, or at least how Uncle addressed them. They were delighted to make my acquaintance, and all three shook hands with me.

Every Sunday they would first have a quick cup of tea; then Uncle would say to me, 'Okay dear, now you go and play'; and all four would lock themselves in his study. Sometimes I would put my ear to the door and listen, sniffing at the fragrance of the incense they were burning inside. I was utterly mystified by what I heard. Peculiar thumping noises, strange voices I was at a loss to recognize, loud exhortations to various people ('Jimmy Dorabji', 'Gool Palsetia', 'Ardesar Irani') to grace their table and make themselves available for questioning. I heard many amazing things. But mostly I heard only silence, and I was soon bored by this game of eavesdropping.

One day, I heard my father's name called out. Then I realized that what they were doing—trying to make contact with that other world, the better world, to which the dead passed away. I heard Bapsymai repeat her invitation three times:

'Bomi Marker! Will you agree to answer our questions?'

As you can imagine, I was waiting eagerly for his reply. In my head, I could hear my father's voice. He was asking me to squeeze his legs and toes, which were aching after a long day at the office. But from the room behind the door, there was only silence. Later on, when I questioned him about these Sunday meetings, my uncle admitted, rather reluctantly, that they were trying to communicate with those of their friends who had passed into the world of the dead. 'We know that nothing ever dies. And if we could share their experience . . .' He explained that what they were doing was called 'holding a séance'. But he absolutely refused to allow me to be present at one.

When the séance was over, Uncle and his three friends emerged from his study looking very thirsty and tired. Bapsymai, heaving and walking very slowly on very high stiletto heels (she was only slightly taller than me even with them on); Fardoon Umrigar drenched in sweat, and Ghauswalla's round shiny face beaming like a full moon. Then we sat down to the traditional Sunday meal of dhaansaak, fried fish and kachumber. Pheena served us, her large eyes turned downward as she handled dishes and spoons with extreme caution as though she could not trust herself not to drop them. At Sunday lunch she was always anxious. She was not like that when we were alone. Then she would chat with me for hours on end in her plaintive, sing-song version of the Parsi Gujarati my uncle and I spoke.

She knew the language because she had grown up there,

working for my uncle. Her mother had worked there before her and died in that same back room which was Pheena's room now. A small cubicle of a room with a window overlooking the backyard where the neighbours chucked their garbage. There was no furniture in this room; only her bedding rolled up in a corner and a large rusted trunk which contained most of her belongings. A mildewed calendar with pictures of the saints hung on the wall beside a Sacred Heart encased in glass; beneath it was a tray on which she lit small, slim candles every evening. Here we sat in the evenings, after returning from our walk in the municipal playground, while my uncle said his prayers in the front hall in a loud, rasping voice, spectacles low on his nose, straining to read the words in a tattered prayer-book.

Sometimes I would sit on her trunk and she would sit on the floor between my knees and let me comb her hair which was shiny and slippery with coconut oil. Sometimes, while I plaited her hair, she would sing for me soft songs in Konkani. Her room, her hair, her brown body carried an odour I had never smelt before. I recognized it as alien, a smell that had no connection with my universe, the world of Parsis that I was familiar with. Did it come from the oil in her hair, the half-dried linen hanging for days on the clothesline in her room, or the patched sheets rolled up in a corner which had soaked in the sweat of every nightmare, perhaps a mixture of all these? Undeniably, it was a smell I associated with sadness, and I longed to know what made her such a strange, unhappy creature. Pheena and I were friends.

There was a bald patch just over her forehead on one side,

which was thinly covered by the hair from above. We shared a private joke about it. I would ask her, 'Pheena what happen to your hair? Hey baldy, where it went?' And she would pull a long face and groan, 'What happen? Rat came at night. Eats up my hairs. Rat hungry, ouch, ouch, ouch, rat wants to eats up all my hairs . . . Ouch, ouch . . .' And start tickling my ribs. My giggling was infectious and delighted her.

But one day, while sitting with Uncle in the hall after he had finished his prayers, on an impulse I asked him how Pheena had lost a patch of hair like that. He frowned and waited to see if I really wanted him to reply. Then he told me, 'Well, you see, many years ago . . . Pheena was very sick. Poor girl, she was in great pain. She could not bear it . . . She pulled it out herself . . . Many years ago that was . . . Not something to talk about. She's probably forgotten . . . Here,' he said, pulling out half a dozen chicken soup cubes from the pocket of his dressing gown, which usually contained toffees, 'tell her to boil some soup for you.' He paused, then said: 'And look here, Soli, shut your door at night, if you want . . . Sometimes in her sleep, Pheena gets up and walks around the house. You might get a scare if you wake up in the middle of the night and see her wandering about like that . . .'

That night, after dinner, I made my way to Pheena's room down the long corridor. There was no light on. A candle flickered beneath the Sacred Heart. For a moment, I thought she might be out. Then I saw her small figure kneeling, her elbows resting on the trunk, her hands clasped together. She may have been praying, but she was shaking with sobs. I went up to her and touched her hair.

'Pheena . . .'

She raised her face to me, streaming with tears, looking like the pictures of the saints in her calendar. Her look disturbed me; I thought, why is she looking at me like that, so pleadingly, as if she were asking my forgiveness for something?

'Why do you cry, Pheena?'

Her lips trembled and she said in the voice of a frightened child, 'I don't know . . . I don't know why I cry . . .'

~

One evening, during my third month at Happy Home, Pheena left me alone at the park to play with the other children. Rather, for them to play around me. I was pretty much older than all the rest. I would be eleven quite soon. In fact, that's why Pheena had left me and gone to the market, because Uncle Framroze had given her a long shopping list, even though my birthday was still a whole week away. Mummy was invited for the occasion, and Uncle's three friends. Maybe some others, too. He was planning a grand lunch.

When I tired of the swings and of balancing myself against the combined weight of three babies on the see-saw, I sat down on a bench. A man approached and stood rather aggressively before me. I had seen him before in the park. Pheena had pointed him out to me. He was the one they called Bokha.

'So *you* are Framroze's nephew,' he demanded angrily of me.

I nodded.

'What's your name?' he barked.

'Soli.'

'Who gave you permission to sit on the swing? How dare you sit on the see-saw! Don't you know they are meant for the children? You're a grown-up fellow, man. What if you break them?'

He had pushed back his shoulders and was glaring at me. Then, he grabbed my wrist in a most menacing way. I uttered a laugh and twisted my hand free. It was a shrill laugh, only half-afraid. He was such a comical, gnome-like figure, all skin and bones, he couldn't frighten anyone; yet he did manage to look rather dangerous.

'Well, I don't think they would break so easily,' I replied caustically. 'And if I'm grown-up, then what about you? I saw you on the see-saw day before yesterday.'

Bokha started laughing and squeezing my arm in a most friendly way, 'That's good. That's a good boy, Soli,' he said, congratulating me. 'I was only testing you. Honest. Honest to God. Don't be angry with me. I was only trying to find out if you have some guts, or you're just a namby-pamby. That's all, believe me . . .' He paused for breath and perched himself on the edge of the bench. 'Courage is the greatest thing in the world. If you have it, you can go anywhere, do anything, nothing and no one can stop you. A boy like you has to learn to be brave. That's what. You don't know me, but I know you. I'm Bokha,' he said, extending his hand. I was getting to rather like him.

'People say all kind of things about me,' he continued. 'Let them say. You ask Seraphina about me. She knows me very well, your Seraphina. I have courage, too. I have real courage . . . People can say anything. But if I'm pushed too far, watch it.

There is nothing I cannot do. Don't push me, that's all. If it comes to that, then just watch me. I am capable of anything. Anything!' He tried to look menacing again. 'I can even slit your throat!'

And he did just that, drawing his thumbnail across my throat with a snarl. Then, with a straight face, he folded shut the imaginary knife and slipped it into his pocket. And further, as if letting me in on a secret of utmost importance, he whispered,

'My bark is worse than my bite though.'

Drawing back his lips and contorting his features, he exhibited to me a rather depleted and misshapen set of teeth, while making a low growling noise from the base of his throat. I giggled, and he continued to pull the funniest faces showing me his teeth from all possible angles. Until I could not hold back my laughter anymore and he joined in with a curious hiccupy kind of gurgling. Suddenly, he challenged me:

'Let's have a bout of panja!'

He threw himself on the ground on his stomach, and stuck out his elbow, placing it firmly on the ground. He wanted to hand-wrestle. I stretched myself out, too, and willingly fell to the challenge. We were in the throes of an intense, well-matched battle when Pheena returned.

'Chi, chi, chi! Rolling on the ground!' she exclaimed and gave Bokha a good dressing-down. Apparently she had asked him to keep an eye on me. She dusted my clothes with her hand, then looked at her wrist-watch.

'Why don't you go play with the other children? It's still early . . .' she said. I wandered away. When it grew dark, and most of the other ayahs were getting ready to return home with the children, I saw Bokha move up close and link his hand with Pheena's.

~

Not until my penultimate week at Happy Home did I realize how close to Uncle's place Bokha and his mother lived.

It was a Sunday afternoon. When Pheena had finished laying out all the dishes for us on the table, Uncle asked her to go and eat. The morning's séance had been a great success but had run on too late. It was already two o'clock, and everyone at the table was ravenous. After a certain amount had been tucked away in silence, Bapsymai initiated the conversation.

'How is she, then, these days?' she asked my uncle in an undertone.

Uncle hurriedly finished chewing a morsel and declared, 'You've seen the rings under her eyes. She won't sleep. She wanders from room to room, like a ghost. I had pills prescribed, but they don't work.'

Umrigar piped up: 'These pills are very bad for you. On the contrary, two spoons of honey, some brandy, hot water . . .'

'Pills won't work, Framroze,' said Bapsymai meaningfully, ignoring Umrigar's interjection. 'I've given you my opinion more than once. In the first place, hers was not a genuine case of possession at all. It was *her* mischief. You know who I'm referring to. We won't mention her name at the dinner table. If we hadn't realized it soon enough and taken precautions . . .'

'But what would be the reason for her continued interest in her?' inquired Ghauswalla learnedly. He seemed to be speaking for my uncle, who nodded and asked, 'Why should she prey on the poor girl?'

'Do you know how often she is with *him*?' Bapsymai continued. 'They're always together in the evening. Ask him,' she pointed to me, 'he must see them together in the park. She wants her to be his plaything—so *he* can be hers!'

All this was too confusing for me. But upon reference being made to my presence, Uncle was reminded of it and he brought the conversation to a halt. But not before Fardoon Umrigar piped up again in his peculiarly thin voice:

'Her days are numbered. But even on her deathbed she hatches her plots and mumbles her foul mantras. . .'

After the meal, my uncle's friends left and he settled down to his usual Sunday nap. The house was quiet again. From the kitchen came the faintly reassuring clatter of dishes. Pheena was washing up. Then she too went off to her room to rest.

The afternoon was hot and still. Outside my window the street was completely dead. Not even a crow or a stray mongrel in sight. The heat bounced off the asphalt paving around Happy Home and hung in the air. On the hillside nothing stirred except a few wisps of smoke, where a family of construction workers had built a fire and cooked a meal. The sky was unbearably bright.

The stillness became so oppressive I could not lie in bed anymore. I wandered out into the front living-room and, for a while, messed around with Uncle's Chinese Puzzle which was really just an intricate game of checkers, boring to play alone. I leaned out of the balcony and gazed at the deserted road tapering down the hill. A curious sensation crept into me that something wasn't quite as it should be. In the low wooden house diagonally across the street at the corner of Sorabji Lane, first among the series of lanes that converged on Forjett Hill—it couldn't be seen from my bedroom, but I'd always believed it to be unoccupied—one window was open, and the curtain raised. At the window sat the fattest, ugliest old woman I had ever seen in my life. She was staring directly at me. I felt uncomfortable, but only for a moment. That was how long it took me to realize that she could not see me. Because this must be the purblind Khorshedmai, whom Pheena had told me about, and that dark, hunched figure, the shape of his head unmistakable, was her only son, Bokha.

His skinny figure had entered the room and was tip-toeing behind Khorshedmai, very stealthily. She must have heard him, because she turned suddenly and shouted something at him. This had the effect of turning a spring loose in him somewhere, activating him, like a clockwork toy: he began to dance around her in a circle, lunging at her, but only from a distance, as if some invisible barrier prevented him from coming closer. He was shaking his fists at her. She sat quite still. Then the curtain was pulled down.

That night I dreamt of my father. He was eating potatoes, wolfishly swallowing them whole. He must have been famished. I saw my mother's tearful face as she served him more and more potatoes, trying to keep pace with the peeling, singeing her fingers because they were steaming hot. I heard voices shouting in the corridor outside my door. I saw the purplish blue night-lamp glowing silently, mysteriously watchful, intense in its brief circumference of light. When I woke up in the morning, I found my bedroom door shut and bolted from inside, as I had left it the night before. But as if in vindication of my troubled sleep, there was a terrific row that morning and Uncle Framroze became hysterical and excessive in the rebukes he directed at Pheena.

When Uncle had opened the front door that morning and bent down to pick up his newpapers, he found instead a coconut split in half, its kernel black and rotten. Around the two halves was a ring of red chilli powder. Within the ring was a sour lime that had been quartered and stuffed with more powders, yellow and vermilion in colour. The sight of this unholy concoction had filled Framroze with terror and he screamed for Pheena and called her names for a quarter of an hour. She began to cry. He warned her that if she was ever seen with that Bokha again, he would pack her off to the home run by the nuns. When the sweeper had come and cleared those things—for he dared not touch them himself or let Pheena touch them—Framroze sprinkled the doorway and the four corners of every room with holy bull's urine of which he maintained a small bottle in his personal wardrobe. Then he began telephoning Bapsymai, Fardoon and Ghauswalla to inform them of the new development.

(iii)

Bokha's desperation grew with every hour that passed. He *had* to do something, he *had* to save her . . . But what? How? A whole week had gone by. With inexorable certainty, the night of the full moon was approaching. Just six days ago, it had seemed infinitely distant, possibly altogether avoidable. Why did I not face the truth? Why did I waste so much time, he asked himself?

That Sunday afternoon, six days ago, Bokha had lost his temper with Khorshedmai. He had grown fiercely out of control. It had frightened him later on, but also charged him with the elation of recklessness. Now see what had come of it . . .

She had insulted him. His mother. Her abuse was no more vicious than usual. But Bokha had lost his temper and spat on her. He had performed his dance of rage before her, lunging at her, always keeping outside the range of her wild snatches in the air. She was too slow, her arms were short and heavy. He had told her he was going. Packing up his things and leaving forever. She would have to pick up her own bedpan from now on. Or she could piss in her drawers for all he cared. Because he was going. He was going away to marry his ayah. He had found a room for them. They would live together happily there, his ayah and he, and he would never come back to see her, not even when she was dead. And she could keep her money which she had hidden away under her arse for so many years.

His anger expended, Bokha realized with a shock that Khorshedmai had believed every word he had said. The outburst was so unlike him; he hadn't known himself capable of it. She had sat in her chair, panting heavily; her face was pale. The blind white flecks in her eyes were expressionless as ever.

'Very well,' her voice had grated hoarsely. 'So she has given you the courage to defy me. At last this Bokha has become a man. Or has he? We'll see . . .'

Her voice had broken but she had never lost her cool.

'So you're challenging me? Very well. I take up your challenge.

Get out! Empty-handed, be sure. Get out. And don't come back, tonight or any other night. The door will be locked to you from now on. As for the girl, I'll see to her.'

Bokha's voice had cracked with incredulity.

'You'll see to her? You? You, who can't even walk to the toilet for a piss? What can you do? Don't give us any more of your empty threats.'

Something like a smile had flickered on his mother's rubbery lips. 'The night of the full moon is only a few days away.' She had muttered to herself.

Her voice was low. But her words had made Bokha break out in a cold sweat.

'When the moon is at its height, I will do such a thing as will completely turn her brain. She won't know what happened. But her mind will go. Then she'll make you a good wife, the slut.'

Bokha had left the house white as a sheet, without saying another word. Had he imagined those tears, the wetness on those cheeks? He would have thought those eyes had hardened to marble long ago.

In the evening, he had returned and quietly inserted his key in the latch. It wouldn't turn. He had clicked it in the slot a few times, then hammered on the door, shouting 'Mumma! Mumma! Open up!' There was no sound from inside. He had spent the night on a bench in the garden behind the fire temple.

In the morning, it had been the same thing. She would not answer. He had spoken to her for ten minutes through the closed door, pleading, making wild promises, confessing it had all been a lie; begging for her mercy. Then he had kicked the door twice and walked away. When he returned to the fire temple, he had found Framroze waiting for him in the porch.

Framroze had caught hold of his collar, shaken him violently and warned him that he would go to the police and asked him to warn his mother as well. Bokha had recoiled in horror when he heard what Framroze had found on his doorstep the previous morning. He had bent and clutched Framroze's feet and sworn that he knew nothing about it. But he was trembling. There was no doubt now that she meant to carry out her threat.

And yet, how cunningly the human mind defends itself against eventualities it cannot bear to acknowledge. Bokha had always believed implicitly in stories he had heard about his mother's maleficent powers. Now he made light of them. What can she do with her coconuts, her chillis, her lemons? The whole thing was laughable. Let her try her worst, he would see her in hell before he let her bend a single hair on Seraphina's head.

~

Bokha had just received his month's salary. He began to spend a lot of time in Gustasp's bar. He bought drinks for strangers and beleaguered them with stories about black magic, spells, wax dolls with needles stuck in them and such like, in order to prove that the whole thing was hogwash. Not everyone gave him the confirmation he sought. One elderly man, a quiet, hard drinker told him a story of a spell that had been cast on his niece, which made her refuse to eat or sleep. She would have died, if the mischief had not been countered by a tantric sorcerer whose services the family employed. A most remarkable man . . . Bokha had stopped listening. He was feeling sick in the tummy. He left his drink and went out into the sunlight.

As a child, Bokha had rarely seen doctors. His mother ascribed all forms of illness—from diarrhoea to the common cold—to the workings of an evil eye which had latched on to her son like a hook. She took her own measures to repel the envy at the root of his sickness. After sunset, a brazier of hot coals was prepared in which a mixture of alum, camphor and rock salt was cooked. When it had boiled to a certain temperature, the ingredients of this mixture would begin to permute, and acquire strange shapes and colours, and a sharp, unnameable odour would overwhelm their rooms. Bokha would stand beside his mother transfixed, staring at the curious shapes the alum would begin to take; shapes suggestive of distorted human or animal figures, heads, faces, noses, eyeballs, lips—the grotesquerie of an entire evil universe condensing in a brazier of hot coals before his very eyes.

One of the few memories of his father that Bokha still retained was of him holding a handkerchief to his nose, eyes streaming behind glasses in the smoke-filled room as he stood obediently beside his son, muttering a private prayer. Bokha tried to remember if her magic had worked. He wasn't sure. Often, his illness seemed to subside the day after the coals were finally quenched. His father at least had never questioned the validity of this procedure. But right through the ceremony, his face would remain puckered in a grimace of distaste.

The remembrance of hot coals lit up another memory in him, of another night. This was later, after his father died. One evening, his mother had returned home unexpectedly early and found him with his pants down, masturbating. She had prepared the brazier then, and branded him on his right arm with a red-hot iron. The crinkled patch of burnt skin still itched every time Bokha had a premonition of some disaster. It was itching now. Unbearably.

God help me. What a wretch I am. Sitting here all day getting drunk. Coward. Do something. What? Well, you tried to act too smart, inventing all those lies about yourself and Seraphina. On the spur of the moment too. And now . . .? Ah, come off it. Nothing's going to happen. The night of the full moon will pass like any other. Mumma will cool down and let you in again. Meanwhile, enjoy this little spell of freedom . . . Bokha went back into the bar and ordered himself a quarter of naarangi.

~

At the end of four days, Bokha had run through his salary. He was no longer very welcome at Gustasp's, especially during peak hours. He hadn't bathed or changed his clothes in all that time and people complained about the pungent odour emanating from him. On the morning of the fifth day, Bokha was climbing up the stairs of Jer Mansion, going up to his mother's flat to routinely bang at the door, when he heard it open and shut quickly, and the latch turn. Someone was coming down the stairs.

It was Soma! He should have known. What was that rascal doing here? Bokha waited for him to come down.

'E-he-he-he-he,' the boy burst out laughing on seeing Bokha. 'Aae Bokha, how does it feel to be a real tramp? Without a roof over your head?'

'What are you doing here?' demanded Bokha. Soma was the local toughie among the neighbourhood servants. He worked for the Karanjias, and was known to have a special rapport with Khorshedmai for whom he did odd jobs.

'What's the matter, don't I do chores for her?' asked Soma insolently.

'What does she want now?' asked Bokha.

'Why, a whole list of things for a new recipe she's trying out,' the boy replied. 'What's it to you?'

'Soma, I'm warning you. She's up to some mischief.'

'Mischief? Your ma's just living it up, Bokha. She's turned you out and now she's planning to have a feast. Celebrating. Who would want to live with a Bokha like you? E-he-he-he-he,' the boy giggled. 'She's even asked me to buy a cock for her from the market for tonight. A live one. The live ones are always more tasty. E-he-hehe-he . . .'

'A cock!' gasped Bokha. He grabbed Soma by the shoulders and tried to shake him, his own body trembling as he screamed, 'Don't you dare, don't you dare!' The younger, muscular boy knocked Bokha's hands off his body with one upward swat of his arm and gave him a slight push.

'Aae Bokha! What's the matter with you? Can't bear to see your ma eat cock?'

Then a funny thing happened. Bokha started crying. He dissolved into tears of helplessness. Soma chuckled and patted his shoulder.

'O Bokha, come on. You're crying, she's crying. Only a minute ago your mother was sobbing away to me,' he said. 'She's afraid you'll leave her. Who'll look after her then? She's an old woman, after all. Go on, make up with her. She'll forgive you.'

'She was crying?' Bokha ceased sniveling when he heard this.

'Swear on God. You think she's happy without you?'

Bokha ran up the stairs like a madman and hammered at the door for a while. Then he pleaded with his mother with renewed earnestness, begging her to let bygones be bygones, he even started to say that if she wanted, he would never again—but there he stopped himself: he didn't say it. And from behind the door, there was nothing: silence.

'Mumma!' he screamed. He kicked the door. Then he spat on it. And walked downstairs again.

All those restless hours he had spent in the past four days came rushing at him again. He had wasted precious hours. Something *had* to be done, quickly. He had to save Seraphina. He couldn't trust his mother to be kind. Seraphina loved and cared for him. He loved her, too, decided Bokha. If this night passes without event, I *will* marry her.

Should he go and fall at Framroze's feet, tell him what was going on in the house across the road? But Framroze had warned him never to show his face again. He might not even give him a chance to speak. Besides, what could the old man do to stop Khorshedmai? Call in the cops? Maybe he should just explain everything to Eruchsaa, ask him to pray for Seraphina and protect her soul. But would Parsi prayers work for a

Christian ayah? Eruchsaa would probably not believe a single word and give him a thrashing in the bargain.

Then, for a second, Bokha's mind was illumined by a small filament of hope. It hung on the slender thread of the memory of a bar-room conversation. That man, the other day. Who was he? He had spoken of a sorcerer, a tantric who had the power to repel spells. Where was he? How could he be contacted? Why hadn't he been listening more carefully? . . . Virar. Yes, that's what he had said. Somewhere in Virar, the farthest suburb of Bombay, lived this sorcerer. What was his name? He couldn't remember it now, though the man had mentioned it . . . But he could go there and ask. A person like that would surely be well-known in his neighbourhood. He decided to set out at once.

As he caught the north-bound train from Grant Road station, he remembered: 'Motilal . . . Ah, yes . . .' That was the name he had overheard.

~

The train was jam-packed. Bokha found himself stranded fairly close to the exit, at a loss to prevent himself from being flung out by anxious commuters who charged the exit every time the train halted at a station. Every new wave of passengers boarding the train pushed him back inside once again, crushing him against a solid wall of people. His cap was knocked off and trampled underfoot. Finally, Bokha managed to wedge himself between two men standing to one side, against the handrail. After a while, the one in front of him glared into his eyes from a distance of about four inches and said rudely, 'Stand straight, can't you?'

Bokha, whose fingers had just been crushed under the hard sole of a shoe while trying to retrieve his cap, lost his temper.

'What d'you mean stand straight! *You* stand straight!'

Just then, the man behind him gave him a shove and moved out. The other man, curiously, seemed to lose interest in the argument and looked away, muttering, 'A mad bawaji from somewhere . . .' At the next station, he too got off.

Virar. The name hooted in his ears, while the train raced to its terminus. What was he to do, he wondered, when he finally arrived? He wandered for a few minutes on the platform looking for the exit. He chose a road that led away from the shops and residential areas, in the direction of vast stretches of marsh. He walked briskly, like a man who knew his business.

It was still early in the evening, but there were few people on the road. Every few minutes, a crowded public transport bus would speed past him, raising dust. For a long while, there were no more buses. Then the street lamps came to life. How do I find Motilal, how do I find the sorcerer? The question kept jogging his brain, but while he had been nearer the station among people, he hadn't known whom to ask, how to ask, and had kept walking, as if he knew exactly where he was headed. Now there was no one around to ask.

By the side of the road, an old destitute woman in rags had made a small bonfire, over which she was warming her hands. This seemed quite strange to Bokha since it was not a cold night at all. He stopped before the fire and waited till the old crone looked up.

Bokha said, 'Motilal . . . Do you know Motilal?'

The old woman made no reply and lowered her head again. Bokha repeated his question. She shook her head and gestured to him to move on. Bokha walked for another half hour. Then he saw a colony of makeshift huts by the side of the road; in one of them a Petromax lantern glowed brightly. It turned out to be a paan-and-cigarette shop. The vendor was an old man with white hair. A bright full moon had risen in the sky. Bokha stood before his kiosk, speechless.

'What do you want?' asked the old man, abruptly.

'Motilal . . .' he muttered, half under his breath.

'Who? Motilal? Motilal who?'

Bokha shook his head. The man understood.

'Motilal Jadoogar?'

'Yes, him,' cried Bokha, much too loudly.

'What do you want with him?' the man asked Bokha, narrowing his eyes a little.

'I . . . I want to meet him.' What else could he say?

'You have a problem?' the old man inquired.

'Yes . . .'

'I'm sorry, he's not here anymore.'

'Where can I find him?' Bokha cried urgently.

'Not in this world . . . Motilal disappeared three years ago. A body was found chopped to pieces among the gravestones of the cemetery next to the dargah. Some said it was Motilal, that he had met an adversary more powerful than he . . . I knew Motilal. He owed me some money. He owed everybody. But he was a good man. He helped a lot of people too . . . I don't expect we'll ever see him again.'

The old man wanted to talk, find out more about Bokha's particular difficulty.

But Bokha's mind had turned vacant. He didn't know any more why he was standing in front of that paan-shop in the wilderness, asking after a man called Motilal, whom he had never met before and now never would. Bokha turned away without thanking the old man. He began walking back towards the station, the way he had come.

Only when he arrived at the station and reached for his wallet to buy a ticket (because he knew ticket collectors lurked at Grant Road station at this hour to nab the ticketless) only then did Bokha start crying. It was not there. His wallet. He felt for it a dozen times, but it was gone. Those two on the train. Stand straight indeed, you bastards! Bokha choked with frustration and his body shook with sobs. Anyway, there had only been five rupees in it.

When he reached Grant Road by the last train, he felt defeated but much calmer. He remembered to leave the station through the siding along the tracks, where the fence was broken. He walked homewards up the incline of Forjett Hill, though what sense it made going there he could not say.

Gustasp's bar had shut. It was too late, even for a Saturday night. Bokha trudged slowly, dragging his feet. God in heaven, what was that? A light on in the flat at this hour? What could that mean? Bokha didn't want to know. He wanted to flee. Something warned him to get out. But he forced himself to climb the stairs, as noiselessly as he could.

Bokha stood outside the door quietly and listened. There was dead silence. He fumbled for the key in his pocket. His hands were trembling so much he had difficulty inserting it in the latch-hole.

The key turned. He pushed the door open a few inches.

'Come in. I was waiting for you.'

His mother was sitting up in bed, eating. There was nothing alarming or unusual about the scene that presented itself as he stepped into the room. Everything was as before. What was more, she had spoken to him kindly. A great flood of gratitude and relief drenched his fraught, embattled nerves. He could have cried.

'Mumma . . .'

'Come. You haven't eaten, have you?' said Khorshedmai. 'Have some of this.' Bokha tried to make out what was on her plate.

'What's that you're eating?' asked Bokha, suddenly tense.

'Cock.'

'Oh . . .' Bokha was silent.

'Eat some.'

'I'm not hungry.'

His mother continued to eat, chomping heartily at a bone. Bokha sat down on the bed near her feet.

'Mumma . . .' He began, contritely.

'Yes, Bokha,' said Khorshedmai. 'I've decided to forgive you. You can come back home now.'

'Oh Mumma, I'll never speak to you again like that. I'm so sorry,' Bokha genuinely was. 'I was so worried. . .'

Khorshedmai continued to chomp.

'I was so worried something would happen . . . That you would . . .' muttered Bokha.

'Worried-burried, forget,' said Khorshedmai, putting her plate aside, looking satiated. 'Come and eat something now. Here. Wipe up what's left in the pot.'

Bokha was overwhelmed. He did something he had not done in many years. He hugged his mother. He threw his arms around her and kissed her.

'Mumma, you're so nice . . .'

'Yes, yes. Now watch—my hands are dirty,' said Khorshedmai, pleased. He buried his head in her vast bosom and let it rest there. Until she rumbled, 'Enough now.'

Bokha helped himself to a leg-piece from the blackened pot on the table beside her bed. He bit into it.

'Mmm. Nice. Bit tough . . .' He chewed at the meat slowly. 'I was really worried. Thank God, she's safe.'

'What did you say?' asked Khorshedmai coldly.

'That girl, you know . . . I thought something would happen . . . Oh Mumma, I don't know what to say. You should meet her . . . I'm so sorry I caused you all this pain . . . But she's really quite a nice girl . . .'

Bokha didn't see her hand move. *Thack!* The slap nearly knocked him off the bed.

'What kind of fool do you take me for?' screeched Khorshedmai, hoarsely. 'Ungrateful wretch! I said I was willing to forgive *you*.'

Bokha stood up, trembling.

'Go. Go in there,' she said. 'Take a look . . .'

'What . . . What have you been doing . . .?

In an instant, Bokha was in the kitchen. On the floor, a circle had been inscribed with red and yellow powders. In it, a large kitchen knife, and the severed head of a rooster lying in a half-dried patch of blood. He became aware of her coarse laughter from the next room, grating on his senses.

'So you saw?' she called out. 'I always keep my word. . .'

The ocular mists in her eyes seemed to gleam with perverse delight. Through their haze, though, she saw Bokha re-enter the room.

Then the room turned red.

~

It was my birthday, and the morning of my last day at Happy Home. Mother was coming over for lunch in the afternoon and then she would take me home with her. School would resume in just two days.

My uncle and I had finished breakfast and were still at the table when the doorbell rang thunderously. Someone had held his finger to it. Framroze and I stared at each other, paralysed. Both of us had a premonition of disaster. But it was Pheena who ran to the door and flung it open. Bokha entered and collapsed in her arms. He was a ghastly sight. The front of his shirt was stiff with blood.

She sat him on a chair in the passage and caressed his head. He was blubbering,

'I got her. I got her *first* . . . She tried to make *me* eat it. In the end, *I* made her . . . eat cock!'

He giggled, and said something even more incoherent. Then he laughed again, and within a few moments it became clear to all of us that Bokha was far away in another world.

Seraphina continued to caress his hair, a remote sadness in her eyes. After a while, she began humming softly, some meaningless plaintive drone of mourning which seemed to soothe Bokha.

Framroze was on the phone to the police when we heard a loud tramping on the stairs. It was Bapsymai, Fardoon and Ghauswalla, come early today for their morning's séance since guests were expected for lunch. In all the shock and commotion, no one had heard the honking of the car. My uncle had never been so glad to see his friends as he was that Sunday morning.

All this happened a very long time ago. When I was in my last year at school, Uncle Framroze suffered a massive stroke which left him paralyzed. A few days later, he was dead. He had provided generously for Pheena, but she donated her entire pension to the Holy Mother's Convent which she joined as a lay kitchen worker. As for Bokha, try as I did, I was never able to find out what became of him, and whether he was still alive. The police hadn't maintained proper records of the case of an old Parsi woman on Forjett Hill Road who was stabbed with a kitchen knife fifty-two times.

Acknowledgements

Percy was first published in *Bombay* magazine's special Short Story edition of 1985; *Unexpected Grace* was first published in *Society* magazine's annual of 1991; *Finely Chopped Dill* was first published in *Gentleman*, January 1997; *Late for Dinner* was first published in *Fulcrum,* February 1976; *Bokha* was first published in *Vox 2* (*Gentleman* magazine's anthology of new fiction ed. by Jeet Thayil), 1997; *Two Angry Men* and *Passion Flower* have never been published before.